INDUSTRIAL CHEMISTRY

MAXWELL PRESS

INDUSTRIAL CHEMISTRY

Clerk Ranken D.Sc

MAXWELL PRESS

Chennai　　　　Trichy　　　　New Delhi

MAXWELL PRESS

This edition has been published in india by arrangement with Carson Books, UK

ISBN 978-81-8094-315-7   Maxwell Press

All rights reserved   No. 44, Nallathambi Street,
Printed and bound in India   Triplicane, Chennai 600 005

MJP 972   © Publishers, 2023

Publisher   C. Janarthanan

Publisher's Note

The legacy of a country is in its varied cultural heritage, historical literature, developments in the field of economy and science. The top nations in the world are competing in the field of science, economy and literature. This vast legacy has to be conserved and documented so that it can be bestowed to the future generation. The knowledge of this legacy is slowly getting perished in the present generation due to lack of documentation.

Keeping this in mind, the concern with retrospective acquiring of rare books has been accented recently by the burgeoning reprint industry. Maxwell Press is gratified to retrieve the rare collections with a view to bring back those books that were landmarks in their time.

In this effort, a series of rare books would be republished under the banner, "Maxwell Press". The books in the reprint series have been carefully selected for their contemporary usefulness as well as their historical importance within the intellectual. We reconstruct the book with slight enhancements made for better presentation, without affecting the contents of the original edition.

Most of the works selected for republishing covers a huge range of subjects, from history to anthropology. We believe this reprint edition will be a service to the numerous researchers and practitioners active in this fascinating field. We allow readers to experience the wonder of peering into a scholarly work of the highest order and seminal significance.

MAXWELL PRESS

CONTENTS

INTRODUCTION

THE precarious state of affairs which existed at the outbreak of war owing to the dearth of certain absolutely necessary materials, and how the difficulties were surmounted, is a story that cannot be repeated too often. The successful efforts made to provide these vital substances are well known to chemists ; but it is desirable that the essential facts should also be brought home to the general public, if adequate recognition of science is to be secured in the future.

It has been proved without doubt that national life is to an extraordinary degree dependent on the chemist, and that nations neglecting science, and most especially applied chemistry, are treading the path which leads to industrial decay.

Germany's success in industry was fostered by a liberal supply of trained chemists and engineers, adequate plant and capital, and co-operation between manufacturers and research workers. Unlike the state of affairs in this country, their business men had some knowledge of science, and their scientific men some acquaintance with business.

We were heavily handicapped by permitting the control of our educational interests to pass into the hands of those who despised a first-hand knowledge of science, and with whom the caste of classics held supreme sway. Science with no voice in our representative Government disqualified one for holding high public office, and the more important positions in the Civil and Diplomatic service could only be counted on with some degree of certainty by those men who lived in the classical atmosphere.

At the same time the treatment of chemical subjects by the daily press is one long series of lamentable blunders committed by unqualified writers and editors, and inflicted upon a public which undeniably fully appreciates any trouble taken to increase its store of knowledge.

Yet, in spite of these disadvantages, Great Britain has become since the autumn of 1914 a larger producer of explosives, pharmaceutical, photographic, and other essential chemicals than Germany. Chemical science furnished the means for that revolutionary change, and the whole land became one vast chemical laboratory. Trade research associations have been promoted by the Government, and, provided purely official administration is reduced to a minimum, British industry should benefit thereby. Scientific men, manufacturers, workers, and the training schools have co-operated, resulting in the establishment of whole groups of new industries. Seeing that " Gott strafe " this, that, and the other industry is not likely to be mitigated in the future, it behoves us to do our utmost to prevent reversion to the old order, with its neglect of science, which slowly but surely leads to national downfall.

The present outlook is encouraging, and, considering the recent headway made, we see the promise of a brilliant future for our science—Industrial Chemistry.

INDUSTRIAL CHEMISTRY

CHAPTER I.

CATALYSIS AND CATALYSTS.

ON glancing into any of the journals published by the various chemical industries, one cannot but fail to be impressed by the constant occurrence of the names " catalyst " and " catalysis." Apparently in every branch of chemical industry the manufacturer is making extensive use of these so-called catalysts, or catalytic reagents, to bring about or speed up many of his processes. Recognizing the fundamental importance of these terms, it seems desirable that we should at once endeavour to get some idea of what they stand for. To those who still remember their Greek, the significance of the term catalyst is obviously an agent which unloosens or sets free something else.

There are enormous numbers of chemical reactions which begin immediately the bodies concerned are brought into contact with each other. On the other hand, it is quite possible to mix certain substances together without any transformation taking place.

Yet the presence of various other agents is able to cause these seemingly dormant mixtures to burst into activity. Such agents which assist or apparently possess the power of commanding the action to go forward are named catalysts, the action itself being called catalysis. The catalyst apparently acts as a stimulant. But the most striking fact, and the one which makes the phenomenon remarkable, is that the catalyst alters neither in amount nor in chemical composition, and can be used over and over again. Some examples will make the matter clearer.

If we mix the two gases hydrogen and oxygen at ordinary temperature, they display the utmost indifference to each other, and may be kept for an indefinite period without the occurrence of any combination. If we now introduce a small quantity of the metal platinum, either in the form of foil or in a finely-divided condition, the gases at once attack each other, the platinum begins to glow and gets red hot, and eventually the action becomes so rapid that an explosion takes place, water being produced as a result of the reaction. The platinum is found to be unchanged at the finish of the operation, and can be used indefinitely to induce the same combination. The method of working of several of the automatic gas lighters on the market is based on this catalytic property of finely-divided platinum. Coal gas on an average contains 50 per cent. of hydrogen. Accordingly, when a gas jet is turned on, hydrogen is thus allowed to mix with oxygen, the latter gas being one of the constituents of the atmosphere. If the gas lighter is so held that the mixed gases impinge upon the portion which contains the platinum, the platinum, as in the example above, becomes hotter and hotter, and finally the temperature rises to the point when ignition of the coal gas takes place.

The smallest trace of the catalyst can effect the transformation of indefinitely large amounts of the reacting bodies. Here, then, we have a wonderful source of power. Its action has been compared to the influence of oil on rusty machinery, or to that of a whip on a lazy horse. It is still a matter of controversy as to whether the catalyst can actually start as well as modify the velocity of a reaction. In the cases where the substances remain in the absence of the catalyst without action, it is assumed that the transformation is going forward indefinitely slowly.

Catalysts do not always bring about combination, many being employed to bring about decomposition. The clear liquid which goes by the name of hydrogen peroxide, under ordinary conditions, is breaking up slowly into water and oxygen, a decomposition which becomes extremely rapid on addition of a small amount of platinum sponge. Here again the metal remains unaltered. Other catalysts may be used to slow down an operation, and in this case are termed negative catalysts.

Everywhere in manufacturing operations we come across processes which must be considered as operating under the influence of these mysterious agencies. One very important case of catalysis in chemical industry is embodied in the " contact " process employed for the manufacture of sulphuric acid, or oil of vitriol. The history of the process, which is rapidly replacing the more cumbrous lead chamber method, reads like a romance, with the catalyst playing one of the chief characters. Difficulty after difficulty was encountered, only to be overcome, the struggle finally concluding with the triumph of chemical investigation. One of the chief steps in the operation consists in the combination of the oxygen of the atmosphere with sulphur dioxide, the well-known pungent gas produced when sulphur is burnt in the air. The union of the two gases produces sulphur trioxide, which with water gives sulphuric acid. Catalysts are employed to bring about the union, the most successful in this case again being finely-divided platinum. Other substances can be, and are actually, employed as substitutes for the platinum, but none of them display the same efficiency. The process was at one time actually abandoned, owing to the fact that the platinum soon lost its magic power, and the continual use of fresh metal was prohibitive owing to its enormous cost. However, investigation revealed the fact that this " sickening " was due to the sulphurous gases containing small traces of arsenic compounds, the effect of which was to poison the catalyst and destroy its activity. If care was taken to remove these traces by cooling and spraying the gases with water, it was found that the platinum continued indefinitely performing its duties.

One must not imagine that platinum is the only one or the chief of a limited number of catalysts; the probability is that there is no substance which cannot under suitable circumstances act in that capacity. The large group of substances termed acids can in certain cases exhibit this property. When cane sugar is dissolved in water, the sugar and water have nothing to say to each other; but if a small amount of hydrochloric acid, or spirits of salt, be added, the sugar and water at once interact, giving rise to the formation of two new sugars, glucose and fructose, while the acid remains undiminished in amount and unchanged in properties. Different acids bring about the above reaction at different rates.

Extremely important are the catalysts grouped under the title of enzymes, which play a very prominent *rôle* in nature. Before the insoluble constituents of foodstuffs can be assimilated, they require to be transformed into soluble products. Certain enzymes secreted in the alimentary canal appear to be able to carry out this transformation. In fact it is not going too far to say that physiology is becoming more and more a branch of catalysis. They are of the utmost importance in the fermentation industries, and it was in this connection that the first was isolated—namely, diastase—from barley malt in 1832. Diastase has the power of converting the insoluble starch of the barley into several soluble substances, one of which is a fermentable sugar. Other enzymes can transform the sugar so obtained into alcohol and carbonic acid gas. Such is zymase, which has been shown to be the active principle of yeast. Most of the enzymes are sensitive to heat, and all are destroyed, if water is present, at temperatures under that of boiling water. The very complex nature of their composition makes their study laborious, and this is rendered doubly so by the difficulty experienced in isolating them. Like other catalysts, they possess the striking property of being paralyzed by poisons; and perhaps it is not too much to hope for, that when we discover the secret of their working as they play their part in the processes taking place in living tissue, we may get some light on the great secret—life itself.

Explanations of catalysis, ranging from those of the present-day scientist back to that given by Berzelius, who first drew attention to the phenomenon, have been far from satisfactory. There are fashions in chemistry as in other lines, and the views concerning catalysis held to-day may be absolutely unfashionable to-morrow.

After this brief description of the power of the catalysts, one can readily comprehend the important position they hold in the realm of economics. If by means of their aid industrial processes can be carried out in less time with a saving of labour, and at a lower temperature with its saving in fuel, the resulting increase of output and lowering in costs are obvious. Practically every industry described in this small volume calls in their aid. Continual research is carried on for their discovery—a research which is everlasting; for, following the discovery of one catalyst, further investigation is made towards getting a better: and if that does not seem fruitful, modification of the conditions can at least be discovered which will bring about improvements in its working. Illustrating this, we have a very modern line of investigation which concerns itself with the search for promoters or activaters of the catalyst. Thus, in the manufacture of nitric acid ammonia and air are rapidly led over different catalysts, which bring about the conversion of the ammonia into the acid. In the process as carried out to-day the catalyst usually takes the form of an electrically heated platinum net. Several of the base metals have been from time to time considered as substitutes for the platinum, most attention being paid to iron. Now pure iron certainly acted as a catalyst, but not so efficiently as platinum. It was eventually discovered, however, that the iron could be activated by the addition to it of small amounts of other metals, such as copper, tungsten, and bismuth, and the results most decidedly showed that satisfactory yields could be obtained without the use of platinum.

CHAPTER II.

ACIDS, ALKALIES, AND MISCELLANEOUS.

Sulphuric Acid, Oil of Vitriol, or Oleum.—Sulphuric acid can unhesitatingly be declared to be the most important of all chemical products—a very king among them. Its uses are literally innumerable, and the amount consumed by a country may be taken as a fair measure of its civilization. Great Britain alone produces over four million tons yearly. About 60 per cent. of the output of the chamber acid is consumed in the manufacture of the fertilizers ammonium sulphate and superphosphate of lime. Along with nitric acid it may be described as the life blood of the explosives industry, while enormous amounts are used in the manufacture of dyes, washing soda, glucose, etc.

Although oil of vitriol was known as far back as the thirteenth century, its commercial preparation may be said to date from its manufacture by Ward, at Richmond-on-Thames, about 1760. At that time glass vessels were employed, but a few years later glass was substituted by lead, the use of which has continued to the present time. The chemical facts on which the manufacture of the acid is based are simple. By burning in air either sulphur itself or such substances as iron pyrites and zinc blende, which contain sulphur as part of their composition, the pungent gas sulphur dioxide is produced. A combination of this gas with the oxygen of the air results in the formation of sulphur trioxide, which on being added to water gives sulphuric acid. Whatever method is employed for its production, the essential part of the process is the combination of the two gases oxygen and sulphur dioxide—a union brought about under the influence of various catalysts. There are two competing methods employed for the production of the acid: the lead chamber method, and the so-called " contact " process. The lead chamber method has long been threatened by its more modern rival, but apparently there is room for both. It has now been established that the contact system is most efficient for the preparation of high strength acid, while for low strength acid, for convenience and ease of working, the chamber plant has the advantage.

The Lead Chamber Method.—This process is carried out in chambers, from three to five in number, made of lead, formerly supported on a structure of wood. In more modern plant the wood has been replaced by a skeleton framework of steel built in with brick, while more intensive working has resulted in a gradual reduction of the chamber space.

Iron pyrites, sometimes termed " fools' gold," is a mineral built up of iron and sulphur supplied to us chiefly from Spain. This ore is the main source of our supply of sulphur dioxide. It is burnt in suitable burners, the air being supplied by a fan blast. Dust and traces of arsenic are removed in a wash tower, and the purified sulphur dioxide, together with air, is led into the Glover tower, down which nitric acid and nitrated sulphuric acid are trickling over flints. As it passes up the tower it carries with it certain nitrous gases derived from the nitric acid and nitrated sulphuric acid. In company with these nitrous gases, destined to play the part of catalyst, it enters the lead chambers. At the same time steam or water sprayed in the form of a fine mist also enters. We have then sulphur dioxide, oxygen, and water ready to be organized by the nitrous gases as they drift through the chambers. The exact method by which the nitrous gases act as catalyst is not definitely settled, but the resulting effect is to combine the oxygen and sulphur dioxide to form sulphur trioxide, which with the water present gives sulphuric acid. Those reactions take place as the gases are carried from chamber to chamber, getting thoroughly mixed in the process. The acid and excess of water condense, and collects on the floors. The excess air carrying the nitrous gases is not allowed to escape, but passes up the Gay Lussac tower, down which sulphuric acid trickles over coke. The nitrous gases are absorbed by the sulphuric acid, producing the previously mentioned nitrated sulphuric acid. This is transferred back to the Glover tower, where it gives up its nitrous gases, which are thus carried back to the chambers again. In this cycle some of the nitrous gases are lost, but the deficiency is made good by the nitric acid which accompanies the nitrated sulphuric acid in the Glover tower.

The problem of concentrating the acid is of great importance, and various plants have been devised for the purpose. The chamber acid reaches a strength of about 70 per cent., and is first concentrated by evaporation in leaden pans. In this way 79 per cent. acid is obtained—a stronger acid attacking the leaden evaporating pans. Such acid is brown in colour, due to organic matter, and is usually termed " B.O.V." (brown oil of vitriol). Further concentration was formerly effected by heating in glass and platinum stills, but the use of such vessels has practically been abandoned. The cascade system of concentration is one of the most popular at present. In this method the weak acid is evaporated in a series of basins arranged in step formation, whereby the acid flows from one to the other, and gradual concentration takes place as the hottest part of the flue is approached. The vessels are composed of fused silica, or acid-resisting material of a metallic character, the upkeep of which is a heavy item.

Another system of concentration is carried out in a Galliard tower. The hot gases, obtained by burning producer gas, are led up the tower, meeting in their ascent a fine spray of the weak sulphuric acid which has been injected at the top.

The Contact Process.—Although the subject of many patents, it was not until 1901 that Knietsch demonstrated the conditions necessary for commercial success. The method was discovered by the Englishman Phillips in 1831 ; but nothing came of the discovery, for, as is well known, in this country there was little sympathy between learning and manufacture. The idea was enthusiastically borrowed by the Badische Anilin and Soda Fabrik Company, in Germany, who after many years of failure saw success in 1901. In developing the process the " Badische " had in mind not so much the displacement of the lead chamber process as the obtaining of a huge supply of concentrated acid intended for consumption in the synthesis of artificial indigo.

The chemistry of the process is practically identical to that of the chamber method. Briefly, sulphur dioxide is combined with oxygen of the air by bringing the gases into contact with various catalysts. The resulting mist of sulphur trioxide with water forms sulphuric acid.

The chief difficulties met with were the ensuring that the catalysts were not thrown out of order. Harmful agents are carefully removed from the sulphur dioxide and air before the mixed gases reach the catalyst. Arsenic bulks largely in the picture, owing to its baneful influence on a platinum catalyst. If sulphur is used as the source of sulphur dioxide, little trouble is experienced in that direction, as the sulphur contains little or no arsenic. But if iron pyrites is burnt to produce sulphur dioxide, volatile compounds of arsenic accompany the gas, owing to arsenic being a constant impurity in that mineral.

In the actual process the sulphur dioxide and air are cooled, purified, and dried before reaching the catalyst. As a rule more than one catalyst is made use of in the operations. Ferric oxide is first employed to bring about a union of about 60 per cent. of the gases, which are afterwards passed on to the finely-divided platinum in order to complete the combination. The resulting mist of sulphur trioxide, no doubt, produces sulphuric acid when added to water. But if this were done, difficulties arise owing to the mist being absorbed with great difficulty by the water. However, 97 per cent. sulphuric acid rapidly absorbs it, forming 100 per cent. acid. Water is constantly run into the condensing tanks at such a rate that the strength of the acid is maintained at 97 per cent.

In the different types of plant considerable trouble has been met with, chiefly during concentrating operations, owing to a certain amount of heated acid escaping as a fine mist, with irritating and disastrous effect. The means of countering this were imperfect until the introduction of the Cottrell electrical precipitating plant. The first of these was erected in this country in 1917, and has proved very successful, not only by the removal of a nuisance, but from the value of the acid recovered. The general principle of electric precipitation depends upon the fact that if a metallic plate is connected to one terminal of high voltage, and a needle-point connected to the other terminal is brought opposite the plate, any solid or liquid particle in the gap between the two takes up a charge of electricity, and is attracted to the plate and condensed there. In the removal of the sulphuric acid fumes the electric potential maintained between the electrodes is 68,000 volts.

The gases enter at a temperature about 80° c., and the amount of acid recovered averages twenty-five tons of 50 per cent. acid per twenty-four hours. The precipitating process, as evolved by Professor Cottrell in 1906, has a field of application extending in every direction. Thus, in metallurgical works lead is recovered from the waste gases of lead furnaces ; dust, formerly a nuisance, and now a source of profit, is abstracted from the waste gases from cement works ; while white arsenic is extracted from the hot gases given off when arsenical copper ores are roasted in the furnace.

The Soda Industries.

Common Salt, or Sodium Chloride.—Rock salt is found in several localities in Cheshire, Droitwich, Stassfurt, Utah, Galicia, and numerous other places. In this country the salt is usually mined by forcing water into the salt deposits by means of a well made for the purpose. The brine is afterwards pumped to the surface and the liquid concentrated.

Coarse crystals result from slow evaporation at a low temperature, while fine-grained " table salt " is obtained by rapid evaporation just below boiling. Of the impurities present, some crystallize before the salt, while others are left in the liquor after the salt has separated out.

Common salt is the raw material used for the preparation of the other sodium salts, such as washing and baking soda, caustic soda, etc. Hence we find the chief alkali manufacturing factories situated in the salt districts.

Sodium Carbonate, or Washing Soda.—Up to the close of the eighteenth century soda was obtained from certain natural deposits or from the ashes of seaweed. About 1791 the French Academy of Science offered a prize for the best process of making soda from common salt. The method submitted by N. Leblanc was successful, and a· patent being granted, the manufacture was begun on a commercial scale. In the French Revolution his factory was seized, the patent declared public property, and no indemnity being paid to him, the inventor committed suicide.

Leblanc's process held the field for over a century, and it is only recently that it has finally given way to its rival, the ammonia or Solvay process, which appeared about 1870. The by-products of the Leblanc method, hydrochloric acid and bleaching powder, assisted it in the struggle ; but owing to the modern electrical manufacture of caustic soda also producing chlorine and bleaching powder, this last source of profit has now left the Leblanc manufacturer.

The ammonia soda process, first ·successfully worked by Ernest Solvay, a Belgian, depends upon the fact that sodium bicarbonate or baking soda is only slightly soluble in cold water. A very concentrated solution of common salt or brine is contained in a tank, under the perforated bottom of which ammonia gas is introduced, and, rising through the liquid, is rapidly absorbed, the tank meanwhile being cooled. Carbonic acid gas is next forced into and bubbled up through the ammoniated brine. The ammonia is obtained from the gasworks, and the carbonic acid gas from limestone. A thick, milky liquid results, containing sodium bicarbonate in suspension and ammonium chloride in solution. This is drawn off, and the bicarbonate removed by filtration or by centrifuging, while ammonia is recovered from the ammonium chloride in solution by heating with lime. After washing with water the bicarbonate thus prepared may be put on the market as baking soda. If, however, washing soda is desired, the bicarbonate is heated in cast-iron pans, being converted into soda ash, while carbonic acid gas is driven off, which can be utilized again to carbonate fresh ammoniated brine. The familiar crystalline washing soda is obtained by dissolving the soda ash in water, and by slow evaporation allowing the crystals to form.

Soda ash is applied in countless ways in scientific industry, and is used in large quantities for the manufacture of glass and soap.

Caustic Soda, Chlorine, and Hydrogen.—Sodium chloride, or common salt, is a compound of the two elements sodium and chlorine. If an electric current is passed through a solution of salt in water, the salt is split up into chlorine, which is given off at one pole, and sodium, which reaches the other. Metallic sodium is not obtained owing to the water interacting with it, producing caustic soda and hydrogen. The net result, then, of the electrolysis is to produce caustic soda and hydrogen round the one pole and chlorine round the other.

In the various commercial methods employed for

carrying out this process, diaphragms and other means are introduced into the cell to prevent inter-mixing of the resulting chlorine and caustic soda. In the Castner-Kellner method the cell is divided into three compartments; chlorine gas is liberated and collected in the two end sections, while in the middle section a water solution of caustic soda is obtained, and hydrogen gas given off. Simple evaporation to dryness furnishes the solid caustic soda.

Most of the chlorine used in warfare was obtained in this way—the gas, which was very concentrated, being liquefied and stored in steel cylinders.

This is also one of the chief sources of hydrogen, which is now consumed in great quantities in the synthetic preparation of ammonia, and also in the oil-hardening industry. The amount used in aeronautics is comparatively insignificant. Caustic soda is the most important alkali, being used in bleaching, dyeing, in the refining of oils, and in paper manufacture.

Bleaching Powder.—If slaked lime is spread in layers on perforated shelves and chlorine gas led in, the gas is absorbed, and bleaching powder is produced. The temperature must not be allowed to rise too high, otherwise chlorates are produced, which are useless for bleaching purposes. Various forms of plant are employed in the manufacture, but they all contain the essential points of exposing large surfaces of lime to the chlorine and, by continual stirring, of endeavouring to expose fresh surfaces. Similar bleaching substances are obtained if the more costly alkalies, caustic soda and potash, are employed to replace the slaked lime. If the temperature of the alkali is about 70° c., chlorates are obtained which are employed in the manufacture of matches, fireworks, and explosives. The chlorates —for example, potassium chlorate—are usually made by electrolytic methods. In the Castner-Kellner cell described previously, the alkali and chlorine were kept apart by means of diaphragms. If these are allowed to mix, and the temperature is about 70° c., chlorates will be produced, and, in the case of potassium chlorate, will crystallize on the bottom of the cell. Bleaching powder is largely used in the bleaching of cotton goods and paper pulp, for the sterilization of water, and as an antiseptic in the treatment of wounds.

CHAPTER III.

ARTIFICIAL FERTILIZERS : THE FIXATION OF NITROGEN.

In the early ages natural manure was sufficient to meet the demands of the thinly populated land; but as man multiplied and required more and better food, agriculturists were forced to the increasing employment of artificial fertilizers. Apparently there is still room for further extension of their use, for even at the present time the experts may be heard condemning our farmers not only for using them in insufficient quantities, but also for failing to apply them in scientific fashion.

For the purpose of agriculture three types of artificial manures are employed. First in importance are those containing available nitrogen; then comes the superphosphate class; and, lastly, those which contain potash.

Nitrates, ammonium compounds, and nitrolime, or cyanamide, are the usual forms in which nitrogen in a suitable form is added to the soil. In the normal course of events the plant assimilates its nitrogen in the form of nitrates, and if ammonium salts and cyanamide have been made use of, certain bacteria present in the soil convert the nitrogenous portion of those manures into nitrates, previous to its being taken up by the plant.

The most important nitrate is sodium nitrate, or Chili saltpetre, natural deposits of which are situated in a rainless district on the west coast of South America—Peru, Bolivia, and Chili. The nitre-bearing rock, called " caliche," is mined and sorted out. After extraction with water, the solution is re-crystallized, so as to separate the sodium nitrate from the accompanying impurities, a nitrate of from 95 to 98 per cent. purity being readily obtained. It is of interest to note that among the impurities is sodium iodate, from which substance the bulk of the world's supply of iodine is procured.

Out of a total yearly production of nearly three million tons of Chili saltpetre before the war, Germany took about 750,000 tons, whereas the United Kingdom imported only 80,000 tons.

Various calculations have been made as to the life of this field, allowing for an increased use of nitre. For some considerable time, about 1925 was confidently predicted as the period of exhaustion ; but this has now proved to be erroneous. More recent surveys of the district allow anything up to two hundred years as the limit. But whatever the true facts may be, the yield must eventually fail. Recognition of these facts has given considerable impetus to the endeavours to obtain artificially from the nitrogen of the air what is already produced for us by nature.

Methods have been evolved for carrying this out,

and it is probably well within the bounds of possibility that nitrates made from the air by scientific
methods will displace a raw material which has to
be transported five thousand miles. Germany certainly erected before the war immense plant for
their manufacture from the atmosphere, and is now
in the position of not requiring to import the natural
product.

There are at present three methods for the conversion or " fixation " of atmospheric nitrogen in a
form available for plant food :—

(1) By the direct combination of the nitrogen
and oxygen of the air, and the absorption of the
resulting oxides in water or alkaline solutions ;

(2) The direct synthesis of ammonia from nitrogen
and hydrogen ; and

(3) Heating calcium carbide with nitrogen, whereby it is converted into nitrolime, or calcium cyanamide.

The first process depends upon a fact, first shown
by Cavendish in 1785, that oxides of nitrogen and
nitric acid are produced when electric sparks are sent
through air. There are several methods for apply-
ing this fact commercially to the fixation of the
atmospheric nitrogen. Birkeland and Eyde's, used
in Norway, may be taken as typical. An electric
arc is produced between two copper electrodes,
through which cold water is continually flowing.
By means of an electro-magnet and an alternating
current an intensely hot disc of flame six feet in
diameter is secured. The flame is enclosed in a
brick-lined furnace encased in metal, and air is

driven through the disc of flame. The resulting oxides of nitrogen are cooled quickly, and pumped into absorption towers filled with broken quartz, over which water is continually trickling. The water and the oxides combine together to form nitric acid, which can be neutralized by addition of limestone (calcium carbonate), or by sodium carbonate, yielding calcium nitrate and sodium nitrate respectively. The calcium nitrate is put on the market under the name of Norwegian saltpetre.

Probably the most expensive item involved in the commercial process is the cost of electric power, and upon its cheapness depends the possibility of the artificial nitrate competing successfully with the natural product. Where abundant water power exists the cost of electric power is correspondingly moderate. Hence it happens that the chief factories in Europe are found in Norway, Sweden, and Switzerland, while in America they are situated in the vicinity of Niagara Falls.

The second method produces ammonia. This is utilized as a fertilizer when combined with acids in the form of ammonium sulphate and ammonium nitrate.

Until recently, practically the whole of the ammonium sulphate was obtained as a by-product in the coal-gas, coke, and shale-oil industries. When coal is treated in retorts ammonia is given off simultaneously with that mixture of gases we term coal gas. It is separated from the illuminating gas by taking advantage of its excessive solubility in water. The ammonia is extracted from the resulting ammoniacal liquor, and combined with sulphuric acid to form ammonium sulphate.

Chiefly owing to the great demand for explosives during the Great War, chemists had to devise other additional methods for the manufacture of ammonia. Now ammonia itself is certainly of some use in that direction ; but what is more important is that nitric acid can be manufactured from ammonia, and nitric acid is absolutely essential for the production of practically every type of explosive.

As a result of chemical research, the well-known Haber method is now being worked on a commercial scale, the raw materials being nitrogen and hydrogen. The nitrogen is obtained from the air, while hydrogen is procured by a variety of methods from water.

The method employed depends for its success upon the use of catalysts. With a high pressure approximating to 200 atmospheres, and a temperature approaching a red heat, the two gases nitrogen and hydrogen can be induced to unite to form ammonia, by the presence of catalysts such as iron. The ammonia is usually combined with sulphuric acid to form our fertilizer ammonium sulphate.

Although one firm in Germany manufactures annually in this way three-quarters of a million tons of ammonium sulphate, a considerable percentage of the ammonia is converted into nitric acid.

The conversion of ammonia into nitric acid is a large industry in itself, extensive plant having been erected in this country to carry out this process.

When a mixture of ammonia and air is brought into contact with platinum, in the form of an electrically heated platinum wire net, the platinum acts as a catalyst, and brings about the oxidation of ammonia into nitric acid. Other metals are occasionally employed as catalysts to bring about this reaction. Iron is used, and is found to work more effectively if small amounts of other metals, such as copper or tungsten, are added.

In some factories the nitric acid so produced is neutralized by a portion of the unconverted ammonia —a step which results in the production of ammonium nitrate.

The third nitrogeneous fertilizer is nitrolime, or cyanamide. The raw materials necessary for its production are nitrogen and calcium carbide. The latter is probably known to the reader as the substance which furnishes us with acetylene gas when water is added to it. The carbide is manufactured by heating a powdered mixture of lime and coke in an electric furnace. While there is only one factory in Great Britain, situated at Manchester, capable of producing this substance, Norway, with its cheap electric power, manufactures carbide on a large scale, importing the coke or anthracite necessary for its manufacture from this country.

The process employed for the production of cyanamide is comparatively simple, consisting of heating the powdered carbide to a temperature of from 800° to 900° c., and passing in the nitrogen under pressure. Rapid combination of the two substances takes place, the nitrogen being absorbed, and cyanamide results.

The output of the calcium cyanamide factories

amounted in 1917 to nearly 900,000 tons, of which amount Germany was responsible for one-third.

In the soil the cyanamide is probably converted ultimately, after a series of steps, into limestone and ammonia. Superheated steam, under a pressure of several atmospheres, is utilized to bring about the above conversion more rapidly. The ammonia so produced is used to supplement the supply, synthesized · from nitrogen and hydrogen, as described above.

Besides its value as a fertilizer, cyanamide is employed in the manufacture of sodium cyanide, a substance extensively used in the extraction of gold from quartz.

The comparative energy consumption for the different methods for fixing nitrogen is as follows: Birkeland-Eyde, 62; the cyanamide process, 24; Haber, 2. Thus the choice of system is mainly dependent on cheap power or cheap hydrogen.

Phosphatic Manures.—The two chief phosphatic fertilizers are superphosphate and basic slag. "Superphosphate" is the name given to a soluble phosphate prepared from either insoluble rock phosphates or bone phosphate.

Phosphate rock consists chiefly of phosphate of lime, and occurs as "apatite" and "phosphorite" in large deposits in America and other parts of the world. Bone phosphate, as its name indicates, is derived from bones. When bones are heated in retorts a residue, termed bone charcoal, is left. When the bone charcoal can no longer be employed as a decolourizing agent in the purification of sugar, glucose, and oils, it is burned in the air, producing bone ash, which largely consists of phosphate of lime.

The rock phosphate or bone ash is finely powdered, and the requisite amount of sulphuric acid run in. A great quantity of gas is given off, the mass becomes stiff, and finally solidifies. The resulting mass of superphosphate is dried by means of steam, and after being ground is ready for use.

During the war the production of superphosphate of lime greatly decreased, not only because of the difficulty of transporting the raw phosphate, but also because sulphuric acid was more urgently required for munition purposes. In Great Britain the production in 1917 was 495,000 tons, compared with 631,000 tons in 1916.

It will be noticed that sulphuric acid, or oleum, as it is called, is essential for the manufacture of the two fertilizers sulphate of ammonium and super-phosphate—about 60 per cent. of the pre-war production of acid being consumed in these industries. Owing to the erection of new plant to meet the enormous demand for oleum necessary for the production of explosives, there promises to be a post-war surplus of acid, the disposal of which is somewhat of a problem. This has led to the Government being recommended to pursue a vigorous agricultural policy, and to enforce the adequate use of these fertilizers.

Basic slag, which is now being utilized to a larger extent, is a by-product in the basic Bessemer and open-hearth processes for manufacturing steel. Previous to 1878 the presence of phosphorus in an iron ore rendered it practically useless for steel production.   In that year Messrs. Gilchrist and Thomas surmounted the difficulty by inventing a process which retained the phosphorus in the slag. This basic slag, containing phosphate of lime, was largely relegated at one time to the scrap heap or used as road metal. Now, if finely ground, and containing not less than 8 per cent. of phosphoric acid, it is found to be a very effective fertilizer.

It is interesting to note that the great Briey iron-ore deposits in Eastern France were of a phosphorus nature, and, therefore, of negligible value until the invention of Gilchrist and Thomas in 1878. Had Bismarck in 1871 been able to foresee its appearance, it is practically certain he would have annexed the whole of Lorraine. In fact, some authorities go so far as to say that the Great War was undertaken by Germany to take over in 1914 what it had let slip in 1871.

Potash Fertilizers.—Furnished by nature with abundant deposits of potash compounds, Germany had practically a monopoly of those substances, and supplied the whole world. How valuable this privilege was becomes obvious when figures are published, showing the sales of the German syndicate to amount to £96,000,000 in 1913. The average amount imported by ourselves was 100,000 tons, containing 23,000 tons of potash. Faced during the Great War with a potash deficiency, the other nations were compelled to supply their needs from other sources. Small amounts of nothing like commercial importance are obtained from sugar residues, and from the ash of vegetable refuse. Various methods have been proposed for the extraction of potash from the mineral felspar, but so far no process of commercial utility has been produced. More success has attended the recovery of potash salt from the gases and dust of blast furnaces, cement kilns, and coke ovens. Potash is volatile at the high temperature at which these operations are carried on, and can be collected from the dust and gases. It is reckoned that 15,000 tons per annum can be expected from this source. As Britain's annual requirements are only about 30,000 tons, the question is on a fair way to being solved.

The search for sources of potash in America has been more successful than expected. Besides recovering it from blast-furnace dust, etc., considerable amounts have been produced from brines in Western Nebraska, the output of which amounted to nearly 50 per cent. of the total for the entire country.

While the original and better-known German deposits of potash are situated at Stassfurt, in 1904 richer fields were discovered in Alsace, thereby completing the formidable economic weapon wielded by Germany. The original German Potash Syndicate limited the working of the Alsace deposits, after buying enough shares to secure control of these fields. Now, of course, with Alsace no longer German, these rich deposits pass out of their control into the hands of France, breaking the monopoly; and no doubt the competition introduced will have a beneficial effect upon the price of the commodity.

CHAPTER IV.

THE METALS.

CHANGES little short of marvellous have taken place in the art of metallurgy during the last decade. The introduction of the electric furnace has permitted the use of temperatures which were otherwise unattainable, while many important metals are now being extracted from their ores by methods of electrolysis. Recent years have witnessed the advent of the aluminium reduction process, or " thermit " reaction, permitting the production of carbon-free metals and alloys, which are of the greatest value in the manufacture of high-class steels.

Certain metals occur free in nature, and are said to be native. Thus we have native gold, platinum, etc. Iron, chromium, and aluminium are found combined with oxygen, while the metal in another group of ores is found united to sulphur, this being the case with such metals as copper, zinc, and lead.

Iron and Steel.—Though the earliest examples of iron are obtained from Egypt, it was probably in Assyria that the metal was first employed for the production of tools, weapons, and ornaments. The Iron Age in Europe may be said to have opened about

37

1000 B.C., but it was not, however, till the Roman Empire was firmly established that the use of iron became general. Pliny writes in the first century that iron was freely used in agriculture and war. The Germans introduced the blast-furnace method of making cast iron into England about 1500, and its employment spread so rapidly that in 1516 a large iron gun, called the " Basiliscus," had been cast in London. About 1735 Darby replaced by coke the charcoal used in the blast furnaces, and in 1784 Cort introduced his puddling process for making wrought iron from cast iron, and laid the foundation of much of the commercial greatness of Great Britain during the century that followed.

A great advance in blast-furnace practice took place about 1830, when Neilson of Glasgow made use of the hot blast, and effected great economy in the manufacture.

The age of steel may be said to date from 1856, when Sir Henry Bessemer made public his process which revolutionized the trade of the world. Certainly steel had been made previously to this ; but prior to 1856 its production was small, and so costly that steel had never been sold in Sheffield for less than £50 per ton. The chief distinction between cast iron, steel, and wrought iron lies in the amount of carbon present, being greatest in cast iron and practically *nil* in wrought iron.

The chief ores of iron are magnetite and hæmatite, which are oxides of iron; spathic ores, which are carbonates of iron, and if associated with bituminous matter are known as black-band ironstone.

Pig Iron, or Cast Iron.—The ore after calcination is mixed with coke and limestone, and introduced into the blast furnace through a cup and cone arrangement at the top. A blast of hot, dry air is blown into the furnace at the foot, which, once the furnace is started, keeps the contents at bright-red heat. The coke is instrumental in removing the oxygen from the iron oxide, producing spongy iron, which combines with a certain amount of the carbon as it passes down the furnace. The compound, or alloy of carbon and iron, melts at a lower temperature than pure iron, and hence at the temperature reached in the furnace the molten metal trickles down and collects in the well of the furnace below the tuyères, or water-cooled nozzles, through which the blast enters. The limestone is added in order that it may combine with the clayey matter accompanying the ore and remove it by forming a fusible slag which lies on the top of the molten cast iron.

The cast iron contains on an average from 1·5 to 4·5 per cent. of carbon, and also small amounts of silicon, phosphorus, and sulphur. In 1916 twenty-one million tons of iron ore were smelted in this country, producing almost nine million tons of cast iron.

Steel generally contains less than 1 per cent. of carbon, and is, as a rule, produced from cast iron. The cast iron is freed from the carbon, phosphorus, etc., and converted to steel by adding the necessary amount of carbon, so that the mass may contain anything from ·1 to ·9 per cent. of that element, depending upon the kind of steel being manufactured. We have the Bessemer acid and basic processes, and the Siemens-Martin open-hearth processes. In the Cementation and crucible processes wrought iron is the starting-point. Electric furnaces are being used in increasing numbers, and promise to play an important part in the future of the steel industry. The presence or absence of phosphorus in the cast iron settles to a large extent which of the Bessemer processes will be utilized. If phosphorus be practically absent, the acid method is sufficient, while its presence necessitates the basic process. The terms acid and basic refer to the chemical nature of the lining of the furnace in which the process is carried out. The cast iron is run molten into a large egg-shaped furnace called a " converter," holding about ten tons. As air is blown through the molten mass the temperature rises, and the carbon is burnt away. The necessary amount of carbon is then added, usually in the form of an alloy, with iron and manganese, and finally the air blast is turned on again for a moment to ensure thorough mixing. The air blast oxidizes part of the iron to iron oxide, which dissolves in the molten metal, and causes it to become brittle while hot. This is usually avoided by adding a small quantity of aluminium. It is interesting to note that the whole operation lasts only half an hour. In the original process, using an acid lining, the phosphorus and sulphur were not removed during the operations described above. Thomas and Gilchrist replaced the acid lining with one made of lime, which united with and removed the phosphorus as soon as it was oxidized by the air blast. The combination of the lime with the oxidized phosphorus produces the well-known basic slag, now extensively used as a fertilizer. The invention allowed the use of phosphatic ores, which could not previously be utilized in steel manufacture, the phosphorus left in the steel producing brittleness. A demonstration of the process was given in 1879 at Middlesbrough. An army of metallurgists from Germany, Belgium, France, and Austria besieged the town, all being anxious to view the operations. Prior to Thomas and Gilchrist's invention, Bessemer got over the difficulty by using Swedish ore, which contained practically no phosphorus.

In the Siemens-Martin processes cast iron is heated with specially picked iron ore, on open hearths, in furnaces heated by producer gas. The method otherwise is similar to that of Bessemer. Smelting in electrically heated furnaces is making enormous strides. Such furnaces are capable of producing steel superior to that obtained in the open-hearth processes, a result mainly due to the fact that the fusion can be effected in an atmosphere practically free from oxygen with its disturbing influences.

In modern times we have had an enormous development of steel alloys produced for special purposes. It has been found that on alloying with other metals, such as tungsten, chromium, etc., the hardness, elasticity, etc., of the steel are very much improved. Thus the importance of the addition of manganese to steel was recognized as far back as 1840 by Heath, and afterwards by Mushet. A small addition is a deoxidizer, while larger amounts confer on the steel increased hardness, rendering it suitable for burglarproof safes, and such articles as crusher plates for ore mills. In 1916, to supply the manganese, over 5,000 tons of manganese ore were mined in Great Britain, and over 400,000 tons imported.

The use of nickel as an ingredient has increased immensely during the past seven years. The construction of some of the greatest engineering structures of the world would have been impossible but for the presence of nickel in the steel employed. One of the most recent structures is the new Quebec Bridge. Alloyed with steel up to 20 per cent., it enhances the toughness, tensile strength, and elasticity. Nickel ore is found in Norway and Canada. Refineries are rapidly being erected in the latter country to treat the ore, the extraction being rather complicated, owing to the presence of copper, arsenic, cobalt, and other metals.

Nickel is used for " nickel plating " other metals on account of its silvery appearance, and the fact that it does not readily tarnish in air. It appears in several important alloys; for example, German silver has 25 per cent. of nickel, and the rest copper and zinc. Nickel coins contain nickel and copper. In the finely-divided condition the metal is employed as a catalyst in the hardening of oils by means of hydrogen.

Tungsten.—One can hardly emphasize overmuch the enormous importance of this " key " metal in the steel industry. In amounts of from 2 to 8 per cent. it imparts hardness, toughness, and tensile strength to steel, and so renders it suitable for the construction of armour-plate, projectiles, and firearms. Much more important, however, is its remarkable power, when alloyed up to 15 per cent., of rendering the steel capable of retaining its temper and hardness at high temperatures. This property was invaluable in the manufacture of high-speed tools, which could be run while red-hot, and yet preserve their cutting edge. In addition to the above highly important uses, the pure metal drawn out into very fine wire is employed in the manufacture of electric lamp filaments. A small amount of tungsten is mined in Cornwall, the ore, " wolfram," being a by-product in certain tin mines. Burma, Australia, the United States, and Portugal were the largest ore-producing localities in 1916. Prior to the war the ore, although mined in the British Empire, was shipped to Hamburg, and the metal extracted by German firms. As a result, in August 1914 the high-speed steel-makers found that there was barely four months' stock of metallic tungsten in the country to satisfy even a normal demand for tungsten steel. Following a Government inquiry, works were erected, an arrangement made with the Colonial Governments to send all their ore to us, and about a year after we were producing metal of 98·5 per cent. purity, fully 1 per cent. better than the best that German manufacturers sent formerly to Sheffield.

The world's consumption of tungsten ore rose steadily from 4,000 tons in 1906 to 10,000 tons in 1913, and to double the latter figure in 1916.

Molybdenum is another rare metal, which resembles tungsten as a steel hardener. Formerly Australia produced the bulk of the ore, but the United States,

Canada, and Norway are now contributing to the world's supply, which totalled in 1916 about 500 tons of ore.

Chromium is of considerable importance when alloyed with steel, either by itself or in company with nickel. It occurs in the mineral " chromite," a compound of iron, chromium, and oxygen, which, when smelted in the electric furnace with carbon, gives the alloy termed ferro-chromium. It is in this form that the chromium is added to steel to form the chrome steels. Our pre-war production was practically negligible, and we imported our requirements mainly from Norway. As a result of the war the manufacture is now a firmly-established industry in this country. Chrome steel is used for armour-piercing shells, armour plates, and is, indeed, invaluable for the wearing parts of aeroplane engines and gears in motor vehicles.

Acid-resisting Iron.—Previously the manufacturer employing plant which had to resist the action of acids was mainly dependent on glass, stoneware, and the more recently introduced fused quartz. It has now been shown that iron alloyed with from 12 to 16 per cent. of silicon (sand is composed of silicon and oxygen) possesses the remarkable property of being resistant to acids, being scarcely attacked by sulphuric or nitric acid. These alloys, however, have the disadvantage of being brittle, and it has been considered inadvisable to employ the material for large vessels which have to withstand internal pressures above 50 lbs. per square inch. Nevertheless, during the last few years the demand for such alloys has been exceptionally great, and they have certainly been a great boon in the plant employed for the concentration of sulphuric acid, and for the concentration of weak nitric acid produced from the fixation of atmospheric nitrogen.

Zinc.—The metallurgy of zinc, or spelter, is an instance of an industry initiated in England passing into the hands of Germany, and this in spite of the fact that the British Empire produced, and British capital controlled, a large proportion of the world's raw material (zinc blende). For example, the total annual zinc concentrates produced in New South Wales alone amounted to 370,000 tons, containing about 145,000 tons of zinc metal. Practically the whole of this went to Germany and Belgium, who smelted the concentrates and obtained the metal. This state of affairs resulted from no particular economic reason. The Germans had secured their trade by greater business and metallurgical enterprise. As a result, many of the mines in Australia had to close down during the war, because there was no plant available for smelting their produce. In 1918 an arrangement was made whereby the British Government purchased practically the whole of the Australian zinc concentrates during the war, and for a period of ten years thereafter.

The erection of zinc smelters in England has advanced slowly, the chief movement in that direction being the expansion of existing works. In the future America will be able to produce more cheaply and in larger quantity than other countries, since she possesses many smelting works, and has recently developed large deposits of high-grade ore.

The chief zinc ore is zinc blende, which is found associated with many other minerals, the chief of which is galena, or lead sulphide. The ore is first separated from the other accompanying minerals and is then roasted. In this way the sulphur is converted to sulphur dioxide, which is not allowed to escape, but is manufactured into sulphuric acid. The roasted ore is reduced with carbon in various types of furnaces, which are so arranged that the volatile zinc is condensed and collected.

The more modern processes extract the roasted ore with various agents, such as sulphuric acid, and obtain the zinc by electrolysis—that is, an electric current is passed through the solution, using aluminium and lead poles. The zinc is deposited on the aluminium, from which it is stripped and melted. The electrolytic processes have developed so rapidly that many look forward to them ultimately displacing the retort methods.

The chief use of zinc is found in the manufacture of alloys. Alloyed with copper, we have brass ; with copper and tin, we get bronze ; with copper and nickel, German silver results ; while bearing metal is produced by alloying it with tin and antimony. Galvanized iron is iron covered with a protective coating of zinc, to prevent rusting.

Aluminium.—Although clays contain about 15 per cent. of aluminium, no method is known for extracting the aluminium cheaply enough for use on a manufacturing scale. The chief source of the metal is an ore termed " bauxite," from which, by a preliminary purification, aluminium oxide, or alumina, is obtained. The process by which the aluminium is obtained from the alumina is electrolytic. Alumina is dissolved in molten " cryolite "—a mineral found in Greenland—and an electric current passed through the liquid. The cryolite remains unaltered, but the alumina is broken up into aluminium and oxygen. The molten aluminium sinks to the bottom of the cell, whence it is tapped from time to time. The process is continuous, fresh supplies of alumina being added when necessary.

The British Aluminium Company, Limited, whose works are situated near Kinlochleven, consider the future of the industry to be so encouraging that they are developing their hydro-electric power there. The field for development is enormous, the applications of the metal being extended in every direction—so much so that the world's consumption of the metal in 1918 was five times what it was ten years previously. The metal is alloyed with small amounts of zinc, magnesium, copper, and nickel, and in that form is used in industry for many purposes where lightness combined with high strength is desired. An alloy of this kind, taken from a Zeppelin brought down in this country, was found to possess a tensile strength of twenty-five tons to the square inch, as against twenty-eight to thirty for mild steel ; but this was inferior to material afterwards produced in this country. In the future such light alloys might find application in bridge-building. The limiting span of a steel bridge is anything from 2,000 to

5,000 feet, while that of an aluminium alloy is three times as great. Another field of utility is the construction of objects which have to be started and stopped—for example, sewing machines, bicycles, road vehicles, etc. When a heavy vehicle is started or stopped much waste of energy takes place, and this loss would be reduced by use of a lighter material. The alloys are also used in the electrical industry, chiefly for transmission lines, since aluminium, although bulkier than copper, is a better conductor, weight for weight. In this way, if aluminium replaces the copper, there is less strain on the supports holding the wires or cables.

The chief objection to using light alloys is that of cost. Prior to the war aluminium was £100 per ton, compared with £7 per ton for structural steel, and although the price of the metal can certainly be reduced in the future, it can never become so cheap as steel.

Powdered aluminium under certain circumstances acts with enormous energy. Mixed with certain nitrates, it forms the basis of some of the best-known and most modern high explosives.

Finally, but by no means least important, aluminium finds extensive employment in the metallurgy of certain metals. Advantage is taken of its great attraction for oxygen and the tremendous amount of heat developed during the combination. If chromium oxide, for example, is mixed with aluminium powder, the mixture is quite quiescent until the reaction is started on its way by means of certain fuses. The aluminium combines with the oxygen of the chromium oxide, and sets free the metallic chromium, which is melted—almost boiled—by the heat developed (approximately 3,000° c.), and which eventually makes its way to the bottom of the crucible in which the operation is carried out.

Similar reactions take place with other metallic oxides. The mixture of iron oxide and aluminium powder is put on the market under the term " thermit." Thermit has been received in engineering with open arms. The temperature produced by the mixture is so high that the engineer employs it to weld together pieces of iron. For example, he may repair *in situ* such an article as a broken fly-wheel. The thermit is packed round the fracture and ignited. The heat melts and welds together the broken pieces. In addition, the molten iron from the thermit helps to increase the strength of the repair. After solidification the excess of iron can be cut or filed away.

Thermit also made its appearance in warfare as part of the material found in incendiary bombs.

CHAPTER V.

OILS and fats can be divided into two classes: glycerides and non-glycerides. The first class comprises the common animal and vegetable oils and fats which have been shown by analysis to be built up of various fatty acids and glycerine. While glycerine enters into the composition of them all, the acids combined with it vary from fat to fat and oil to oil. The mineral oils, such as petroleum and shale oil, are found in the second class. They consist of mixtures of substances containing various proportions of the two elements carbon and hydrogen.

Margarine.—Till within recent times butter was largely relied upon for the requisite proportion of fat in the human diet; but the supply of butter is now inadequate for the needs of the nation. We apparently are doomed to live in an age of butter substitutes, and accordingly the margarine industry is of some considerable importance.

Margarine looked at from all sides is a product of war conditions, first appearing during the Franco-Prussian War, and developing to an enormous extent during the Great War. The former prejudice against it is rapidly breaking down, and everywhere huge works are being erected in this country to undertake its production, for not so very long ago we were quite content to import from Holland and Denmark the bulk of the margarine consumed. In 1913–14 the average weekly output of the home manufacturers was only 1,500 tons, a figure which by 1918 had risen to over 5,000 tons weekly.

In 1869 a French chemist, Mège-Mouriès, attracted by the offer of a prize by the French Government for a butter substitute, produced from fresh beef fat a substance with a butter-like consistency, and termed oleo-margarine. He later improved upon this product by churning it with cows' milk, getting an emulsion which could be solidified, salted, and coloured to resemble the real article.

In 1887 the Margarine Act was passed, and all butter substitutes had to bear the title " Margarine," and at the time of writing it is necessary to have the word printed in $1\frac{1}{2}$-inch letters.

Since Mège-Mouriès's period the manufacture has steadily improved, and margarine prepared from vegetable oils and fats has come more into vogue, replacing the purely animal fat varieties. About 90 per cent. of the output is now made exclusively from vegetable oils ; but in the more expensive kinds animal fats predominate.

The chief animal fats employed are lard and " premier jus," the latter being obtained from the best beef fat. From the " premier jus " by hydraulic pressure at 48° c., using filter cloths, a fluid oil, " oleo," is expressed, leaving the harder " stearine " behind. Stearine is more solid at ordinary tempera-tures, and is used on this account to counteract the more liquid vegetable oils used, and give the final required consistency. The choice of vegetable oils available for use in margarine production is large ; the most important are cotton-seed oil, palm-kernel oil, and arachis. Of these oils, that obtained from cotton seed, by crushing and subsequent purification, is admittedly unrivalled for the manufacture of margarine, and also artificial lard. In this country the seed is crushed whole, just as it is received, whereas in America it is first shelled, and the kernel alone crushed. The latter method, known as the " decorti-cation " system, produces a purer and more edible oil. The residue of the seed, after removing the oil, forms an excellent cattle food.

Lastly, but by no means least, a very important group of hardened or hydrogenated oils has made its appearance in the industry. The introduction of these hydrogenated products marks a great tech-nical advance. The discovery of the principle on which the process is based is due to Professor Sabatier, who, however, received no share in the pecuniary results, others having taken out patents for the processes involving its application. It is gratifying, therefore, to record the recent award of a Nobel Prize to the professor.

The process is an excellent illustration of cata-lysis. It was discovered that when hydrogen is injected into various oils heated to 200° or 250° c., with a small amount of finely-divided nickel present, the oils combined with the hydrogen, producing a solid fat with a much higher melting-point than that of the original oil. In other words, an oily liquid substance could be converted into a fat, solid at ordinary temperatures. No reaction takes place without the presence of the nickel; it itself remains unaltered, and yet causes the combination to take place.

By means of the process inferior oils, such as whale oil, can be hardened and converted in solid fats, suitable for soap-making. Cotton-seed oil is readily altered to a fat with the consistency of lard. It has been found also that these hardened fats have excellent keeping qualities. An excellent example of the application of the hardening process is seen in the manufacture of artificial lard. Formerly artificial lard was made by the admixture of refined tallow with cotton-seed oil, bleached by means of fuller's earth, the proportion being selected which gave a substance with a consistency as nearly like lard as possible. But since the introduction of the hardening process there is no need to use tallow, the desired result being attained by mixing liquid with hardened cotton-seed oil.

One objection urged against margarine made from some of these hardened oils was that they contained small traces of nickel, and hence might be poisonous. This question has been thoroughly tested, and the small traces present have been shown to be quite harmless.

Milk is also used in margarine manufacture. It is either fresh skimmed or separated, and is required to be of a high state of purity. It must be sterilized. Boiling as a means of sterilization is precluded, inasmuch as the properties of milk are altered and a burnt flavour might result. For the destruction of undesirable bacteria the milk is heated to 82° c.— that is, well below boiling-point—for a few minutes, the method being termed pasteurization. Various other methods of sterilization can be employed, utilizing electrical currents in some cases, and in others the ultra-violet rays.

The actual manufacture of the margarine may be shortly outlined. The milk is first cooled to about 10° c., and then inoculated with lactic acid bacilli, which causes it to sour rapidly, and curd precipitates out. The lactic fermentation imparts a pleasanter taste and aroma, but true butter flavour is lacking. The milk is then churned with the melted mixture of animal and vegetable fats and oils, until emulsification is satisfactory. The temperature of churning is extremely important, from 25° to 35° c. being customary. If the temperature is correct, spotting of the finished margarine by clots is avoided. The emulsion, passing through a valve, is met by a spray of ice-cold water, which causes instant solidification, and at the same time breaks up the mass into yellow granules. These crystals collect in a wooden trough, so arranged as to allow drainage of the water. They are then removed to the maturing room, and the bacteria introduced by the milk allowed to develop. The mass is kneaded to expel the excess of water, the legal limit of the latter being 16 per cent. Finally, passing to the blending department, the mass is mixed with salt, flavouring material, colouring matter, and preservatives. It is interesting to note that the composition of the substance giving butter its flavour has hitherto resisted all attempts at identification, and research in this direction is still required. Sometimes butter itself is added, but this must not exceed 10 per cent. The usual preservative employed is boric acid, and must not exceed in amount ·5 per cent. In some cases artificial milk has been employed in margarine technology, and is a distinct advance.

One of the problems attracting some attention in the margarine industry is the question of its food value, as affected by the presence or absence of vitamines. It has been demonstrated that the growth of animals will not take place unless the food contains minute quantities of certain ingredients, commonly termed vitamines. What these substances are is still obscure, and much work yet requires to be done before we can speak with certainty about them. Butter fat is rich in certain of these substances, while in vegetable fats they are almost always absent. The use of vegetable oils in margarine manufacture has been adversely criticized on the ground that the consumption of such margarine is liable to be attended with malnutrition, and the contraction of such diseases as beri-beri and scurvy.

Soap.—Soap was apparently unknown to the ancients, for we read of garments being washed by mechanical rubbing, aided by the presence of ashes of plants. Nevertheless, that its origin dates back to a comparatively early period in the world's history is shown by the fact that a complete soap factory was found in the excavations of Pompeii. The raw materials necessary for the production of soap are caustic alkali and fats and oils. Tallow, palm oil, and cocoanut oil are largely used ; but within recent years the tendency has been to make it only from such fats and oils as cannot be rendered marketable for edible purposes.

The common animal and vegetable fats and oils, termed " glycerides," are built up of glycerine and various fatty acids, such as stearic, palmitic, and oleic.

Various methods are known by which the oils and fats can be split into glycerine and the acids, the process being termed saponification. Heating a fat with caustic soda brings about this result, with, however, a slight modification ; we get the glycerine, but not the acids, on account of the latter combining with the caustic soda. The combination of the soda and acids produce the substance known to us as soap. If caustic soda is used, the resulting soap is hard ; but if caustic potash be substituted, the product is soft.

In the manufacturing process the melted fat and caustic soda, or " lye," are run into the soap kettle together, while free steam is blown in to mix them and form an emulsion of the oil and lye. The mixture is boiled until saponification is complete. Soap is soluble in water, but its solubility diminishes greatly if salt is also present in solution. Accordingly, salt is added, causing the soap to separate, rising to the top, the under layer consisting of the spent lye and glycerine, the so-called " sweet-water." The sweet-water is drawn off, leaving the soap in the kettle.

In order to ensure the complete decomposition of the fats and oils, more lye is added to the soap in the kettle, and boiling repeated. After allowing to settle, the spent liquor is drawn off, and the soap pumped into a vessel, where perfume and filling materials are added, and the mass thoroughly mixed. It is then run into frames, and allowed to solidify and afterwards dry, and finally cut into bars by different mechanical devices, such as forcing the slab against wires.

Rosin treated similarly to the fats also produces a soap ; accordingly, a large number of yellow soaps are manufactured from the fats and oils admixed with rosin.

The toilet varieties are, as a rule, made from better materials ; but many very cheap grades are produced from poorer stock, and the defects covered by high colour and perfume.

A well-finished soap should contain from 35 to 40 per cent. of water ; but it is by no means rare to find the amount greatly exceeded.

Glycerine.—Glycerine is so closely associated with the soap industry that no soap plant is complete without its department for saving the glycerine in the fats and oils used by the soap manufacturer. The " sweet-liquor " obtained in the manufacture of soap is concentrated, decolourized by bone charcoal, and distilled by means of passing in superheated steam.

Glycerine can, however, be obtained directly from the fat or oil without necessarily producing soap. If the oil is heated with water to which a small amount of sulphuric acid is added, the oil is split up into glycerine and the fatty acid. The sulphuric acid acts as a catalyst, and remains unchanged. Other reagents have been discovered which bring about the catalysis at a lower temperature, or more quickly than the sulphuric acid. One of the best known, termed " Twitchell's reagent," is a complex substance derived from coal tar. The melted fatty acids rise to the surface and float on the top, the liquor underneath containing the glycerine. From the sweet-water the glycerine is recovered. The fatty acids on the surface when cooled may or may not solidify. If the fat gives stearic acid, this solidifies, and is used for candle-making under the name stearine. Oleic acid, on the other hand, is a liquid. If the oil is hardened by the process described under margarine manufacture, the resulting fatty acid can be obtained in the solid condition.

If the acids are not required for the manufacture of candles, they can be neutralized with sodium carbonate, and so produce soap.

Glycerine is utilized for copying-ink, for various medical purposes, and, owing to its resistance to being frozen, finds employment in gas meters. However, the greater bulk of it is consumed in the manufacture of explosives. Treated with a mixture of nitric and sulphuric acids, we get the oily liquid called nitro-glycerine. Dynamite is made by absorbing nitro-glycerine by means of a fine siliceous earth. Mixed with gun-cotton, it also enters into the composition of cordite.

Mineral Oils.—The only actual producer of mineral oil in this country is the Scottish oil industry. By destructive distillation of the shale found in Mid- and West Lothian a crude oil is produced, which corresponds to the crude product obtained directly from the petroleum wells in America, Mexico, Russia, Rumania, Burma, Persia, etc. The Scottish industry has the advantage of the by-product sulphate of ammonia ; but in spite of this it has only been by constant improvements in plant and method that it has held out against the competition of petroleum.

The output of petroleum in 1917 was over 70 million tons, equal to 17 gallons per head of the estimated population of the world. The British Empire furnishes only 2 per cent. of that output— a fact which emphasizes the value of British control in the Persian oilfields.

Drilling for oil can be carried to depths of over one mile. As a rule the oil is pumped through iron pipes from the oilfield to the refineries, which may be situated hundreds of miles distant. At the refineries the crude oil is placed in retorts and distilled, the vapours being condensed in receivers, which are changed from time to time as the specific gravity of the distillage increases. The lighter and more volatile portions, which are collected first, constitute the liquids sold as motor spirit, under names such as petrol. Then comes in order of volatility the solvent naphtha, followed by the fuel and illuminating oils, such as paraffin and kerosene. What is left in the retorts, on heating further, furnishes lubricating oils, vaseline, and the paraffin waxes suitable for candles, leaving eventually a residue of coke.

The production of oil from cannel coal has come to the fore again after more than fifty years' retirement. Such material yields by low temperature distillation fifteen to eighty gallons of crude oil per ton, and the crude oil, when refined, gives at least 8 per cent. of motor spirit and 50 per cent. of fuel oil.

CHAPTER VI.

COAL TAR AND COAL TAR COLOURS.

THE coal tar industry is now recognized to be of fundamental importance, and has been classified according to our modern method of nomenclature as a " key industry." Dyes, drugs, explosives, are all manufactured from the primary derivatives of coal tar. The war has brought it home to us that a well organized coal tar industry is necessary for public defence. Factories producing synthetic dyes from coal tar can easily be converted so as to manufacture high explosives; hence it follows that a well developed dye industry is a very great asset to a country contemplating war—a fact obviously well known to Germany, The whole question is in reality part of a larger problem: the conservation of our fuel resources. The biggest proportion of our coal is burnt in a wasteful manner, no provision being made to collect the escaping volatile products, ammonia and tar. Where fuel is so wasted, one cannot be expected to manufacture cheaply coal tar derivatives.

Coal Tar Primary Products.—When bituminous coal is heated in retorts, the chief products obtained are coal gas, ammonia, tar, and coke. The coal tar when collected is a black, oily, evil smelling liquid, and in the early days became a great nuisance, owing to no use being known for it. The composition of the tar varies within wide limits, depending on the temperature of heating, the quality of the coal used, and on the size and shape of the retorts. Whatever the composition, the tar is, at any rate, a very complicated mixture, having a specific gravity of approximately from 1·1 to 1·2.

The coal tar is subjected to distillation usually in vertical stills arranged in a row, and generally of ten to twenty tons capacity, although in America the charge may amount to double the latter figure. The distillate is collected in fractions, which may be divided up as follows :—

(1) Light oil, that distils approximately at from 150°–220° c.

(2) Creosote oil, that distils approximately at from 220°–280° c.

(3) Anthracene, or yellow oil, that distils approximately at from 280°–350° c., leaving a residue of pitch in the still.

Each of these fractions is worked up and separated into its constituents.

In many ways the light oil is the most interesting fraction, and from it are obtained benzene, toluene, phenol (carbolic acid), and several others of less importance. Benzene and toluene are liquids, while phenol is a solid.

Benzene, the discovery of which is generally credited to Faraday, in spite of the Germans claiming to have discovered it forty years previously, is the starting-point of aniline oil manufacture, and has also been in great demand for the production of synthetic phenol. An enormous amount of phenol is made in this way, owing to the demand far outstripping the production of phenol from coal tar. Treatment with sulphuric and nitric acids converts it into picric acid, used in the high explosive lyddite.

The tri-nitro derivative of toluene, "T.N.T.," produced similarly to picric acid by action of the sulphuric and nitric acids on toluene, was little known in this country previously to the war. Its high explosive power, combined with the comparative safety with which it can be manufactured and handled, caused an urgent demand for it, and consequently for the toluene from which to make it. The history of the Allies' success in producing this German explosive is one of the interesting romances of chemical industry. Sulphuric and nitric acids go to form the life-blood of the high-explosive industry, hardly an explosive being made without their aid.

Creosote oil on being cooled deposits crystals of naphthalene. The napthalene is usually centrifuged, and the residual liquid used as a wood preservative, liquid fuel, etc. Naphthalene is used in the manufacture of many dyes, and is the starting-point of one of the modern methods of making artificial indigo.

On cooling the anthracene oil a dark green powder is obtained, containing 40 per cent. of anthracene, which is purified by means of various solvents. The purified anthracene is the parent substance of the alizarin dyes.

Synthetic Dyes.—The coal tar industry is one of the glaring instances of an industry initiated in England which made far greater progress on the Continent (notably Germany), and contributed enormously to the prosperity of others rather than to the pioneer country. Our lack of progress has been chiefly our own fault. Firstly, we have failed to realize that research work is the soul of industrial prosperity ; and, in the second place, the attitude between the professors of chemistry and the manufacturers has been one of mutual aloofness and reserve. On the other hand, it must not be forgotten that there are economic as well as educational reasons for Germany's supremacy in the coal tar colour industry.

It is questionable whether any other industry has ever furnished such a striking object lesson in the application of scientific research to industrial progress. This branch of industry owed its inception to the accidental discovery of mauve made by Sir William Perkin in the course of a scientific attempt to artificially produce quinine. How enormously the industry has developed is shown by the fact that while Perkin never manufactured more than half a dozen colouring matters during his connection with the industry, the total number of dyes now on the market amount to several thousands. The date of Perkin's discovery was 1856, and from then until 1870 was a period of great activity and considerable prosperity among British colour makers. Our principal competitors were the French. But after the Franco-German War the German factories took the lead, and the period 1870–80 must be recognized as that in which British dye-making was definitely overtaken by the German industry. One of the reasons for this lay in the fact that the German Government gave a liberal subsidy to the scientific colleges out of the indemnity demanded from France. As a result, a race of well-trained chemists was produced, who quickly developed and improved the process of manufacture. Thus, at the outbreak of war Germany was forty years ahead of us. In spite of this, during the last three or four years we have made great efforts, and it is quite possible that in ten years' time we shall again be in a position of equality with Germany.

Intermediate Products in Dye-making.—The direct coal tar products—benzine, toluene, phenol, naphthalene, anthracene, and others of minor importance—are first of all converted into more complex derivatives, from which the colours are ultimately produced. Those complex derivatives hold so important a position that they have been classed, and named " intermediates." Before the war the dye-makers of other nations bought those intermediates from the Germans and converted them into dyes, or purchased the finished dye direct from Germany. One of the fundamental intermediate products is aniline oil, which has always been most extensively manufactured in Great Britain. The first step in its manufacture is to convert benzene into nitrobenzene, which is a pale yellow liquid with the odour of bitter almonds, sometimes used in perfumery under the name of " oil of Mirbane." This conversion is carried out with the aid of nitric and sulphuric acids, and one can hardly fail to notice how the whole path is beset with a continuous demand for those acids. From nitrobenzene one proceeds to aniline, by replacing the oxygen of the nitrobenzene by hydrogen. This is effected by adding iron borings and hydrochloric acid to the nitrobenzene, and the resulting aniline oil is distilled over from the liquid mixture. More modern factories are now carrying out the reduction by passing the nitrobenzene vapour mixed with hydrogen over certain catalysts. Aniline is a colourless liquid, becoming brown on exposure to air. Aniline is also the starting-point of numerous other fundamental intermediates, such as demethylaniline and diethylaniline, which are derived from the aniline by its reaction under pressure with methyl and ethyl alcohols respectively. These are the starting-points of such well-known basic colours as methyl violet, malachite green, methylene blue. Demethylaniline is also vital to the manufacture of certain explosives. The production of the above-mentioned intermediates is now in such a flourishing condition in Great Britain, that we are able not only to supply our own demands, but export to Switzerland, which has always held a position of some importance in the manufacture of dyes. Salicylic acid is another intermediate, important not only to the colour industry, but also for drug manufacture. It is obtained from phenol (carbolic acid) by the action of carbonic acid under pressure. Prior to the war it was not made in this country, but its manufacture is now firmly established. It is said to be the parent of more than thirty-six dyes. From phenol we can by action of nitric and sulphuric acids get dinitrophenol, or proceed farther and get trinitrophenol (picric acid). Dinitrophenol is of the highest importance, being used in the manufacture of sulphur colours, which are consumed in enormous quantities in peace time, and also in war time, for Government equipments. Unlike some of the other intermediates, the manufacture of this particular one was carried on in Great Britain prior to the war. By means of sodium sulphide and sulphur it is converted into sulphur black. Sulphur colours have been produced in larger bulk than any other class of colour since the war broke out. Dinitrophenol is a very good illustration of the close connection between dyes and explosives. It can be converted into sulphur black as above mentioned, while further action of nitric and sulphuric acids converts it into trinitrophenol, the high explosive, probably more familiar under the name of picric acid. It is therefore fortunate that its manufacture was firmly established in this country previously to the outbreak of war.

The story of the artificial production of alizarin from anthracene is well known. Alizarin is one of the main products of the madder plant, the roots of which were used from time immemorial for the sake of the dyes they contain. Originally grown in India and Persia, it found its way into Spain and the

Netherlands; and about 1870 the annual import of it into this country was valued at over a million pounds. The chemist has changed all this, and the cultivation of the madder plant for dyeing purposes is now at an end. Anthracene is oxidized to anthraquinone, and this, by action of fuming sulphuric acid and subsequent alkaline fusion, is converted into alizarin. It comes into commerce in the form of a paste containing 10 to 20 per cent. of alizarin, and is used for dyeing cotton turkey-red. The manufacture of alizarin and allied colours has not hitherto been developed in this country to any great extent. Here nature has imposed an additional handicap on development, due to the fact that practically all the bromine originates in Germany. Bromine is largely used in this branch of colour manufacture.

The industrial results following the successful production of artificial alizarin stimulated chemists to attempt the artificial formation of another natural dyestuff—namely, indigo.

Indigo is one of the oldest of known dyes, probably originating in India, and introduced from there into other countries. The stem and leaves of the indigo plant, *Indigofera tinctoria*, are cut and placed under water; fermentation starts, and a greenish-yellow liquid is drawn off and run into vats. This is thoroughly stirred by workmen or mechanical stirrers, in order to bring the liquid into contact with the oxygen of the air. The indigo precipitates and is allowed to settle, washed, and then boiled to prevent a second fermentation. Finally, it is filtered through cloth and pressed into cakes, and dried out of the sunlight. The natural indigo of commerce is a dark blue solid, insoluble in water. The acreage of ground used in the cultivation of the indigo plant in India shows a rather interesting trend. The area under cultivation was largest in 1896–97 being over 1,500,000 acres, and the yield of indigo over 8,000 tons. The cultivation fell off steadily, until in 1914–15 the total area under this crop was only 148,400 acres. This decline was due to the introduction into the market of the artificial indigo in 1895. The natural product held its own for some time owing to its superiority over the artificial product for dyeing purposes. On the outbreak of war the natural indigo got a second chance, which it was quick to take. As a result, the area of cultivation again rose rapidly to over 750,000 acres in 1916–17, producing almost 5,000 tons of indigo. The authorities have paid attention to the improvement in the seed and type of plant, and have also introduced marked improvements in the methods of manufacture and marketing. For example, they have endeavoured to get over the difficulty of the former variable purity and composition of the natural product which caused the dyer continual trouble. Trustworthy estimates seem to show that it is just possible that the natural indigo will be manufactured and sold at prices at which the competition of the artificial indigo need not be feared.

The manufacture of artificial indigo with naphthalene as the raw material was one of the triumphs of the Badische Anilin and Soda Fabrik Company.

The first synthesis had toluene as the starting-point; but owing to the limited amount of toluene in the world that synthesis was dropped. It would be tedious to detail all the steps by which indigo is evolved from naphthalene. Sulphuric acid plays its part. In fact, the necessity of a cheap supply of the concentrated form of that acid brought the modern " contact " method of manufacture of sulphuric acid into being. The establishment of the industry on a commercial basis was the outcome of close and systematic study by a large number of German chemists, who were subsidized by a company sufficiently courageous to spend enormous sums of money in that manner rather than distribute it as dividends.

Dyeing.—As a rule silk and wool are dyed directly, while cotton and linen, having less affinity for colouring matters, usually require the assistance of what is termed a " mordant." The dyestuffs themselves are spoken of as " substantive " and " adjective." The former colour fibres directly; the latter will only colour permanently when used in conjunction with a mordant. The customary mordants employed are the oxides of aluminium, iron, and chromium. The colouring matter unites with these mordants, forming compounds termed " lakes," which are insoluble in water. Alizarin forms lakes of different colours with the above mordants. That produced from it and aluminium oxide is bright red—the well-known turkey-red; while with iron oxide the resulting colour is purple. The cotton fibres are impregnated first with the metallic oxide—that is, the mordant—and then dipped into the dye solution. The insoluble lake is produced in the fibre of the cloth, making the dye permanent.

The theories of dyeing are not yet completely elucidated, the recent study of colloids and absorption having brought about a modification of the hitherto accepted theories.

CHAPTER VII.

FLAVOURING MATERIALS, PERFUMES, AND DRUGS.

THE preparation of perfumes by extracting them from plants and flowers is an industry which dates back several centuries. During the last thirty years this field has attracted a great number of chemists, who have investigated the constitution of the essences to which the flowers and plants owe their fragrance. Accordingly, we find the artificial products built up in the laboratory competing with the natural products. The perfume in a plant usually resides in what is called the " essential oil." These essential oils usually consist of two constituents, one of which gives the characteristic odour.

Grasse, a mediæval town on the Mediterranean, is the seat of the industry for the extraction of pure natural perfumes from flowers. Throughout the whole year, with the exception of the winter months, the various blooms are being picked. In March and April come the flowers of the violet, while May and June see the gathering of the roses and orange flowers. In the other months, thyme, rosemary, myrtle, jasmine, and lavender, to mention only a few, are ready to be picked and the essences extracted.

Certain of the perfumes are extracted by a process of distilling the flowers with water. The volatile essential oils distil over with the steam, and are afterwards condensed in suitable receivers. The oil floats on the top, and can be drawn off from the condensed water, which also retains a small amount of dissolved essence. This water may be used to distil a fresh mass of petals, but, as a rule, a large amount of it is sold as rose water, jasmine water, etc.

There are, however, certain perfumes whose delicacy is affected by the heat and steam during distillation, and, such as the tuberose and jonquil, have their essences extracted by another method. This method is termed "enfleurage." The flowers are pressed against cold lard held on glass plates in wooden frames. From day to day fresh flowers are laid upon the lard until it is saturated with the essence. According to this plan the perfumed lard has to be melted and strained from the spent blossoms. In the more modern method contact of the petals and the lard is avoided. Moist air is drawn through the flowers, and then conducted over the fatty layers, the lard duly absorbing the perfume. By whichever method the fat is charged, the perfume is extracted from it by shaking with concentrated alcohol; the alcohol being afterwards evaporated and the extract obtained as the "quintessence" of flowers. A variation in the process consists in stirring the flowers in melted lard, and subsequently filtering off the melted lard containing the perfume, leaving the exhausted flowers behind.

According to another plan, which can be applied

to all flowers, light petroleum spirit is employed to dissolve out the fragrant essences, and the spirit afterwards evaporated by distillation in a vacuum. The quality of the perfume as obtained by the enfleurage process is far superior to that extracted by the other methods.

France has long been the home of the industry, and is the greatest producer of natural perfumes.

Such, then, is a description of what has been accomplished by the land. Let us now examine what has been done in the laboratory in the way of production of synthetic perfumes. One of the earliest examples was the preparation of the artificial vanillin. The natural article is the odorous principle of the vanilla pod, the fruit of a species of orchid growing wild in Mexico. To-day it is prepared artificially from eugenol, a comparatively inexpensive substance, the chief constituent of oil of cloves. By a series of steps, employing oxidizing agents, such as ozone, eugenol can be transformed into vanillin.

Ionone is the name given to the artificial essence of violet. It is made from citral, a substance existing in considerable amount in essences of lemon, and in lemon grass oil, to which the characteristic lemon odour of these materials is due. Citral and acetone, heated with an alkali, condense and form pseudo-ionone, which, when boiled with dilute sulphuric acid, yields a mixture of two ionones. Most of the violet products are blends of these two ionones. In these examples the natural and artificial products are identical in composition.

The chemist on other occasions can imitate a

natural perfume, and this is what happens in the case of artificial musk. The synthetic product does not resemble in composition the natural musk obtained from the secretion of the musk deer. There are also a number of examples where the chemist has manufactured an entirely new perfume, which is neither a natural product nor an imitation of the natural article. Heliotropin is a case in point. Mixed with vanillin, it is sold as " white heliotrope."

It is wonderful to find how little the consumption and the price of the natural product are affected by the coming of the artificial products. Its appearance has in most cases urged the natural perfume manufacturer also to enlist the aid of science, and so improve and cheapen his method of production. To get the most delicate perfume, it is essential that the essence be pure. Raw vanillin smells but little ; it is only when purified that it exhales its powerful, well-known odour. Slight impurities have enormous effects.

The essential oils are used to scent toilet soaps, and also, of course, as perfumes. But their consumption is greatest in other forms. Great amounts are employed in making aerated waters and for flavouring alcoholic liqueurs; also in confectionery and cooking. As medicinal agents many of them are included in the pharmacopœias, being used as antiseptics in the treatment of wounds and as parasiticides. Eucalyptus oil is now employed in the treatment of spotted fever and scarlet fever.

Before the Great War a large number of essences

were manufactured exclusively in Germany, and consequently became scarce and costly on the outbreak of hostilities. The urgent demand for essences, such as vanillin, created a supply at home, and the British firms are now manufacturing many in large quantities. This last statement applies with equal force both to the synthetic drugs and fine chemicals generally.

Drugs.—From perfumes and flavouring essences it is an easy transition to drugs. There are several points of similarity. Many drugs are extracted from plants and animals, while others are synthetic products built up in a laboratory. Although Britain had long been a producer of morphine, quinine, strychnine, and emetine, Germany also manufactured those bases, with the exception of morphine, on a very much larger scale. But that is not all. The preparation of the rarer alkaloids, such as atropine, and practically the whole field of synthetic drugs lay entirely in German hands. It is therefore pleasant to record that at the present time we have an industry developing and growing to considerable proportions, and antiseptics, antipyretics, and sedatives of purely English manufacture are now available to medical men.

Quinine, morphine, and strychnine are the active principles in certain plants. These principles exist ready formed in the plant, and are not modified by the treatment in the laboratory, but merely extracted in a pure state by suitable solvents from the vegetable tissues which contain them. For example, quinine is extracted from cinchona bark, morphine from opium, and strychnine from the seeds of nux vomica. The various cinchona barks owe their febrifuge virtues to several alkaloids, of which the two chief are quinine and cinchonine, the latter being obtained as an accessory product in the manufacture of the former. The mention of accessory products recalls the published statement that there are lurking suspicions that British physicians and British patients have been prescribing and consuming synthetic remedies, merely because by chance something occurred as a by-product in a German factory, and an outlet had to be found for it. Let us, however, return to our alkaloids. The cinchona barks, which are cultivated in India, Ceylon, and Java, are finely ground and subjected to a process which concludes with the extraction of the alkaloids by chloroform or petroleum. Quinine sulphate is the salt usually used in medicine. Opium, which is the dried juice of the poppy capsule, contains not only morphine, but also a very large number of other alkaloids, from which it is separated with some difficulty. In spite of elaborate and patient investigation, the artificial production of morphine and quinine remains still unaccomplished. Cocaine is an instance of a drug obtained from natural sources and also made artificially. It is obtained from coca leaves, in which several closely related alkaloids appear. The leaves are extracted with water, tannin, and other substances, precipitated by lead acetate ; the lead removed, and the solution made alkaline ; and, finally, the cocaine extracted from the solution by means of ether. Its hydrochloride is used in medicine as a powerful anæsthetic. Hypodermically injected through a hollow needle, it brings about temporary loss of sensibility to the part, and hence is used in small operations—as teeth extraction. Owing to several fatal cases following its use, it is being replaced by novocaine and eucaine, which are safer.

In the earlier days expeditions were organized to seek out new medicinal plants. The Fiji Islands, the West Indies, and Peru were exhaustively searched, and in this way certain invaluable drugs were obtained. Such was cocaine. But this search is no longer carried out with its old time vigour. The reason is not far to seek. It lies in the fact that from the substances present in coal tar an ever increasing number of new drugs are being artificially produced. Such are phenacetin, aspirin, antipyrine, and many others. If coal tar is distilled, among the products which can be condensed are benzene, toluene, phenol (carbolic acid), and naphthalene. From benzene one can pass by easy stages to the aromatic liquid aniline; and from aniline by five or six steps one arrives at phenacetin. Aniline is also the starting-point in the manufacture of antipyrine.

If the sodium salt of phenol (carbolic acid) is heated with carbonic acid gas, and hydrochloric acid added to the aqueous solution, we obtain salicylic acid. This acid and its sodium salt are useful antipyretics in rheumatic fever. Another important product derived from salicylic acid is aspirin, which is the acetic acid derivative. Aspirin was the proprietary name of the German article, and has been renamed acetylsalicylic acid by its manufacturers in this country.

The drug, salvarsan, affords a powerful illustration of our dependence upon Germany in the days before the Great War. Introduced by the late Professor Ehrlich, salvarsan, or " 606," is of the greatest importance in the treatment of syphilis. At the outbreak of war we had no supply of this potent drug, a state of affairs which was quickly remedied by the actions of a British and also of a French firm. It is a synthetic compound of the element arsenic, but containing it in such a condition that arsenical poisoning is not produced. Needless to say, coal tar derivatives also enter into its production. A number of new compounds allied to salvarsan have recently been brought into use. Caustic soda and salvarsan give sodium salvarsan ; the addition of a copper salt gives copper salvarsan, which is stated to be useful in sleeping sickness. The British firm manufacturing salvarsan supplies it in this country under the trade term " Kharsivan."

Among antiseptics we must mention formaldehyde and phenol, or carbolic acid, the latter obtained, as stated above, from the distillate of coal tar. Formaldehyde is obtained by the oxidation of methyl alcohol, one of the constituents of the spirit derived from wood by distillation. The oxidation takes place on mixing the vapour of the alcohol with air in contact with heated platinum. The platinum acts as a catalyst. Produced in this way, formaldehyde is a gas which is soluble in water. The 40 per cent. solution is sold under the name of formalin.

It is employed in the preservation of milk, a few drops keeping it sweet for several days. With ammonia, it gives urotropin.

Drugs from plants and drugs from coal tar do not entirely exhaust the field. One of the modern branches is engaged in the extraction of drugs from animal organisms. Most success has attended the extraction of the active principles from the so-called ductless glands. So far the only actual industrial preparation of these has been accomplished in the case of the suprarenal gland. Adrenaline was isolated from it by Takamine in 1901, while its artificial production was patented two years later. The quantity obtained from a pair of bullocks' suprarenals is exceedingly small, amounting only to 0·025 grams.

Adrenaline is a light yellow substance, whose solution when injected has a powerful constricting action on most of the small arteries. It stops bleeding, and is most useful in the treatment of most kinds of hæmorrhage. In a like manner the active principles from the thyroid gland and pituitary gland are employed in medicine.

The whole drug industry is one where the skilful chemist is absolutely essential—the methods of preparation are so elaborated, and require much perfection of detail. Moreover, any mistake or mischance in the preparation might bring about fatal results which no amount of subsequent effort could retrieve.

CHAPTER VIII.

THE CELLULOSE INDUSTRIES.

In the realms of modern manufacture the importance of cellulose as a raw material can hardly be emphasized too strongly. It is the key substance of more than one chemical industry, being essential for, and consumed in large quantity in, the making of such varied substances as paper, artificial silk, celluloid, the waterproofing materials used in aeronautics, and lastly, but by no means the least important, the modern explosive gun-cotton.

A plant is built up of microscopic cells. Cellulose has its origin in the walls of those cells, being the skeleton or framework of the vegetable tissue. Linen, which is the fibres of the stem of flax and cotton, which consists of the hair from the seed of *Gossypium*, are well-known forms of practically pure cellulose. Other abundant sources are wood, esparto grass, straw, and, within recent years, bamboo.

Chemists have shown that cellulose is made up of the three elements carbon, hydrogen, and oxygen. But notwithstanding the large amount of investigation recently undertaken on this substance, they have to admit that they are still in the dark regarding the exact arrangement and building together of these atoms.

There are some slight differences between the cellulose obtained from cotton or linen and that extracted from wood. These variations depending upon the origin are, however, of appearance and structure, and not of composition.

The most striking property of cellulose, and the one which the industries employing it take full advantage of, is its resistance to the attack of chemical agents. Neither does it decay when exposed to the action of the weather, and will last throughout generations.

Of these industries, first in importance comes the manufacture of paper. Our civilization exists largely on a paper basis, and to feed the mills which manufacture it, science laid her hand on cellulose, which we cannot make, but only take from plants. Prior to 1866 paper consisted almost entirely of rags. Owing to the consumption increasing by leaps and bounds, new sources had to be looked for, and in that year esparto grass was introduced by Thomas Routledge, while simultaneously an inquiry was undertaken as to the possibility of wood furnishing its quota of cellulose. However, it was not until some years afterwards that the wood-pulp (cellulose) industry was launched.

Different varieties of cellulose are utilized for the different grades of paper. The cheapest qualities, such as that which a newspaper makes use of, are manufactured from mechanical wood pulp. In other words, wood is pounded and smashed up, finally appearing as a sheet of paper. The coniferous woods growing in Norway, Sweden, and on the shores of the Baltic furnish in this country the greater part of this supply. It is reckoned that on an average one of our daily newspapers consumes each day ten acres of forest. Such a paper does not last, for, besides pure cellulose, the wood fibre contains other substances, which are acted upon by moisture and the air, and rapidly disintegrate.

For the manufacture of the better classes of paper, England, in addition to using rags and esparto grass supplemented by straw, also imports chemical wood pulp. Further treatment of the mechanical wood pulp produces the chemical wood pulp which approximates more closely to pure cellulose. After removing the bark, the wood is cut into small pieces and boiled for several hours with bisulphite of lime or magnesia. The cellulose, with its high resistivity, is unattacked, while the non-cellulose portions of the wood are resolved into soluble substances which are washed away. The yield of pulp is from 40 to 50 per cent. After bleaching the mass, which is brown in colour, the resulting pulp is subjected to a process of beating, to separate the individual fibres and bring it into a smooth condition. The fragments are usually one to two millimetres in length, and the fibres are torn rather than cut, so as to get greater felting power. During this operation of beating, the loading, sizing, and colouring materials are added to the pulp. Most papers, with the exception of the finest qualities, have added certain loading materials. These are mineral matters, which are incorporated in the pulp, with the purpose of filling up the pores, and giving the paper a better surface. In the expensive varieties, pearl hardening, which is calcium sulphate, is employed, while in the cheaper sorts china clay is the substance used. The next stage consists of sizing. If the paper is to be afterwards employed for writing, and in some cases printing, it requires the addition of some material to enable it to resist ink. There are two methods of achieving this result, called engine-sizing and tub-sizing respectively. In engine-sizing, resin dissolved in washing soda is added to the pulp, and a solution of alum added. The result is to give a fine precipitate of aluminium resinate, which fills up the pores and prevents the ink soaking into the body of the paper. As a rule, starch is also added in solution, not for sizing purposes, but rather for binding the fibres together. In tub-sizing the finished paper is passed through a solution of gelatine to which alum is added. Soap also may or may not be present. Very often the pulp after bleaching has a faint yellow tint, to correct which ultramarine is very often employed. Very little paper is hand made nowadays owing to the greater expense of labour. However, bank notes and various grades of drawing-paper are still manufactured by that process. The usual paper is machine made. In the machine we have a wire cloth, on to which the pulp streams, giving a continuous sheet of paper. The wet sheet is passed between hot rollers, which dries and finally polishes it.

Wood pulp is, and must always remain, the staple raw material of the world's paper supplies. This is illustrated by the estimates of the paper-making materials imported during the year 1915. Over 500,000 tons of mechanical wood pulp, augmented by 400,000 tons of chemical wood pulp, entered this country, while linen and cotton rags, esparto, etc., together totalled only 200,000 tons. In Canada, which is the richest forest area in the world, the wood-pulp industry has developed very markedly. The official returns for its production in Canada for the year 1915 show a total of over a million tons, which amount is expected to be increased by half for the year 1918.

An important development of paper is its conversion into yarn, which is being exploited very actively in Germany. The yarn is made from paper run from reels and split into strips, which are damped and twisted. Clothing material of fair appearance has been made by alternating wool and paper yarns two by two. While such cloth may have been acceptable as a war-time substitute, opinion as to the permanent status of the industry is cautious, even in Germany. As a substitute for jute in twine or carpet matting, there are greater possibilities, bearing in mind the greater susceptibility of the paper fabrics to damage by water.

Let us now turn to an industry that is as modern as paper-making is ancient. This is the manufacture of the material known as artificial silk, which is now produced in filaments of almost unlimited length, possessing any desired degree of lustre, and of a sufficient tenacity, dry or wet, to be used in any textile operation.

To the enterprise of a French technologist, H. de Chardonnet, we first owe its industrial production. He began to manufacture it in 1891 at the rate of 100 lbs. per day at Besançon, and was producing about 4,000 lbs. per day before anything was made on an industrial scale in this country.

Besides Chardonnet's process, there are other two methods on the market. Of these three methods, viscose silk, the latest, is the only one which is entirely English in origin and development. As in the other two processes, it is a form of cellulose; but, unlike them, its starting-point is not cotton, but wood. It is thought by those most competent to judge that, although its manufacture is more complicated than the older processes, it will ultimately supplant them.

We shall confine our attention, then, to the viscose method. Norwegian spruce is the usual starting material, and the 50 per cent. cellulose which it contains is obtained in a comparatively pure form by boiling the cut wood in a solution of bisulphite of lime under pressure, and subsequently bleaching. The next stage consists of mercerizing the cellulose. This process was first used by John Mercer in connection with cotton, hence its name. He found that cotton when treated with caustic soda shrank, becoming 50 per cent. stronger, and more easily dyed. If the cotton was fixed, so that it was not allowed to contract, it takes on a silky sheen. To proceed, then. The cellulose from the spruce is mercerized by soaking in a solution of caustic soda, the excess soda removed by pressing, and the dry alkali cellulose allowed to mature and afterwards treated with a very volatile inflammable liquid called carbon disulphide. A brown, sticky mass results, rejoicing in the complex chemical name of cellulose sodium xanthate. When dissolved in water or dilute caustic soda it forms a golden brown, thick syrup, and to this, on account of its viscosity, was given the name viscose. This was first produced by Cross, Bevan, and Beadle in 1892. The syrup is decomposed by a large number of substances, and even in water alone it gradually breaks up, the final stage bringing us back once more to cellulose. The viscose is forced through jets into various spinning baths which contain solution, which bring about this coagulation. Sulphuric acid and sulphates, also sodium bisulphite, have been used in this manner. The resulting thread stuff is cellulose, which reappears after the cycle of changes. This is drawn on to bobbins, washed in various ways, dried, and is then ready for the textile manufacture.

The tenacity of artificial silk when wet or dry is by no means as strong as natural silk; yet so great an improvement has been made within recent years, that it will stand wear and washing excellently, and it is in common use for fancy goods, braid, knitted and woven underwear, and dress fabrics.

Of other industrial applications of viscose, the production of a length of transparent film, useful for photography, etc., is a variation on the process described above, the liquid viscose being drawn through a slit $1\frac{1}{2}$ millimetres in width, instead of forced through a jet as above.

Cellulose Acetate.—With suitable treatment cellulose, obtained from any of its sources, will dissolve in acetic anhydride, a substance derived from acetic acid by removal of water. As a result cellulose acetate is produced, and for use is dissolved in acetone. If the solvent is allowed to evaporate, the cellulose acetate is left as a film of great tenacity and high lustre. Under the name of " dope," such solutions have now an extensive use in aeroplane construction, being employed to render taut and impermeable the textile fabric which constitutes the air-resistant surface of the wings. Its application increases the textile strength of the linen by at least 25 per cent. If tetrachloroethane is used instead of acetone as the solvent, the resilience imparted to the aeroplane wing is increased. However, owing to the poisonous nature of its vapour, the use of this solvent has been prohibited in this country. Cellulose acetate itself in sheets one-hundredth of an inch in thickness is strong enough for aeroplane wings, and, owing to its transparency, is almost invisible at a height. It has the drawback, however, that a tear when once started spreads very rapidly.

It is also used for photographic production, notably for the preparation of the continuous cinema picture film. Being a splendid insulating material for electrical wire, and at the same time a varnish for metallic surfaces, its manufacture for this purpose is now an established industry.

Celluloid.—When cellulose in the form of tissue paper is acted upon with a mixture of sulphuric and nitric acids, substances in appearance the same, but in reality markedly different from the cellulose, are obtained. These are the so-called cellulose nitrates. The higher ones are known as gun-cotton, while the lower ones dissolved in alcohol and ether give the well-known article collodion. However, if instead of dissolving in alcohol and ether, the cellulose nitrates be thoroughly mixed with camphor, and afterwards alcohol in small amount added, and the whole mass compressed in a hydraulic press heated by warm water, a plastic substance called celluloid is obtained. The great objection to celluloid is its inflammability, and attempts have been made to diminish this by the addition of substances such as asbestos. It is plastic at 75° c., is easily welded, and lends itself readily to the imitation of a large number of products, such as ivory, marble, and tortoise-shell. It is widely used in the manufacture of combs, brush and mirror backs, piano keys, knife handles, collars, etc.

The question as to who was the inventor of celluloid is still a matter of controversy. Daniel Spill, of Hackney, manufactured it in England under the trade mark of Xylonite; while J. W. Hyatt, of Newark, N.Y., produced it in America under the registered trade mark of Celluloid. Hyatt was led to its discovery while making attempts to discover a substitute for ivory for the manufacture of billiard balls.

CHAPTER IX.

SUGAR is present in the saps of some trees, and in the juices of practically all fruits. At the present time the two main sources in order of importance are the beetroot and the sugar cane. But this was not always the case, for up to as recently as 1880 the sugar cane easily held the first place. The sugar cane grows only in those climates which are warm and moist with intervals of hot, dry weather; while beets thrive best in a temperate climate.

Probably sugar was first met with in India, for we have it on record that in the seventh century A.D., a Chinese emperor sent people to India to learn the art of its manufacture. From China it apparently made its way into the countries round the Mediterranean, and we hear of the Crusaders, when they had returned home, importing refined or loaf sugar into Northern Europe. The Turks in the fifteenth century overran these districts surrounding the Mediterranean, and the sugar industry there was practically extinguished. Meanwhile it had been spreading in other directions, and the colonial possessions of Spain, Holland, Portugal, together with our own colonies, had undertaken its preparation so successfully that, from being a fancy luxury, it had now become an article of common consumption. By the middle of the nineteenth century the countries producing cane sugar in order of importance were Cuba, Java, Mauritius, the British West Indies, and Brazil.

The raw sugar was imported into this country, and great refining factories sprang up in London, Liverpool, Bristol, and Greenock. It is interesting to observe how the imports rose and fell, and the explanation thereof. If we take the case of Greenock, we find that the sugar refineries there imported 50,000 tons of raw sugar in 1854, and that this amount rapidly increased until, about 1880, they were importing nearly 250,000 tons. This was the turning-point, for fifteen years later we find the imports reduced to exactly half that figure, and this in spite of the fact that our sugar consumption had risen fourfold. The yearly amount of sugar used by us had risen to 1,600,000 tons, and let us note the important fact, that of that figure only 129,000 tons came from sugar cane; the explanation, of course, being that by that date about two-thirds of the world's supply was coming from the beetroot fields of Northern and Central Europe.

The success of the beet sugar is a very striking example of the result of energy and persistent scientific research. The origin and rise of the beet-sugar industry to a certain extent may be laid to the credit of Napoleon and the king of Prussia. The blockade of Prussia by the former caused the necessity for the expansion of the home-grown sugar.

Also, naval engagements in the West Indian waters, the sinking of sugar cargoes, the capture of merchant ships from the West and East, and other blows dealt by France at Britain, did not conduce to the well-being of the sugar-cane industry. Germany hit upon the right kind of stimulus to improve the industry. They levied the sugar duty, not upon the sugar produced, but upon the roots. The farmer was at once stimulated to produce the richest possible quality of root, and the manufacturer to extract the maximum amount of sugar from each root. Immense trouble was taken to improve the breed of sugar beet. At first only 6 per cent. of sugar was obtained from the root, but by slow improvement we find in 1908 a beet had been obtained from which as much as 17·6 per cent. of sugar was possible to be extracted. France hastened to adopt the German system, but never succeeded in catching up in the race.

Within recent years the cane sugar producers began to set their house in order, and by adopting several hints regarding methods from their rival, and employing several new ones of their own, they are once more in a position to compete with the beet-sugar industry. The research is still going on, and endeavours are being made to breed new varieties, giving more sugar, able to resist disease, and suitable for various soils and climates.

Various attempts have been made in this country to grow the beet and produce our own sugar. In 1910 a factory was established at Spalding; but the project fell through, owing to want of public support. A later attempt in 1918 promises more success. An estate of 5,600 acres has been acquired at Kelham, Newark, by the British Sugar Beet Growers' Society, Limited, the soil and climate being well suited for the purpose. It is satisfactory to record also that the Treasury has granted £125,000 towards the cost of the enterprise.

The sugar is obtained from the canes by crushing them between rollers, whereby the juice is squeezed out. Instead of having, as formerly, only one three-roller mill squeezing the cane twice, they now employ mills which give the cane eight squeezes. With that and similar improvements they are now obtaining 95 per cent. of the juice. The waste cane pulp is known as " begasse," and may be employed as a fuel. The juice is run into a vessel, and milk of lime added to neutralize the organic acids, and boiled to coagulate albuminous matters. This part of the process is termed " defecation." Any excess of lime may be removed by carbonation, which consists in passing in carbonic acid and getting a precipitate of carbonate of lime. After skimming, the liquid is evaporated down in a vacuum, in the heat-saving, multiple-effect evaporator, until it is so concentrated that, on cooling, crystals of sugar form. The mixture of crystals and syrup is named " masse-cuite." The crystals are now separated from the treacle or molasses by means of a centrifugal machine. Raw sugar so obtained is brown, owing to substances produced from the juice by decomposition during evaporation, and has afterwards to undergo the refining process. Bone charcoal has the property of absorbing this brown substance, and advantage is taken of this fact in the refining. In the refineries the coloured sugar is dissolved in water, and allowed to percolate through vessels containing bone or animal charcoal. The liquid comes through colourless, and is again concentrated in vacuum pans, and the crystals obtained. The loaf sugar of commerce is made by running the magma of syrup and fine crystals from the vacuum pan into conical moulds, where it is allowed to stand for some time. A further crystallization of sugar takes place, which cements the grains together, while the uncrystallized syrup drains off. Owing to slow draining, it is customary to place several of the cones in a centrifugal machine with points outward. The syrup and subsequent wash waters are forced through the mass, which is left as a hard, dry, conical loaf.

Let us now return to the molasses, or treacle. It still contains a large percentage of sugar; but certain substances present prevent its crystallization. A large amount of investigation has been made on the recovery of this sugar. In spite of all endeavours, a small fraction is still left, which cannot be separated in the crystalline form. To the molasses is added a solution of strontia, which forms an insoluble compound with the sugar, which can be removed by filtration. If this compound is suspended in water, and carbonic acid gas passed into the liquid, the strontia is removed in combination with the gas. The filtered liquid is again concentrated, and more sugar crystals obtained. Molasses is sometimes fermented for making alcohol or rum.

A portion may be used as a fuel in the furnaces, and a small amount is absorbed as a cattle food.

The preparation of raw sugar from beets follows more or less similar methods to those employed in the extraction of the raw cane sugar. Slight differences occur chiefly in the method of extracting the juice from the beet. The beets are cut into slices, or shredded, and systematically digested in hot water. The process is called diffusion, and depends upon the fact that sugar and certain crystallizable bodies are able to pass or diffuse through the cell walls of the beet into the water, while the proteid bodies, gums, etc., are retained by the membrane. Thus the juice so obtained is much purer than that obtained by the older methods which employed pressure. After passing through a pulp separator, the juice is treated similarly to that described above in the preparation of cane sugar. The resulting beet sugar, on being refined, produces a substance identical with the sugar obtained from the sugar cane.

Glucose is found in the juices of ripe, sweet fruits, such as grapes, plums, bananas, etc. It also occurs in honey, which is a mixture of several sugars, extracted already formed, from the plant by the bee. Glucose is not so freely soluble in cold water as cane sugar, nor is it so sweet. It is invariably manufactured on the large scale from starch, as the most convenient raw material. By boiling starch paste with dilute sulphuric acid, it is converted into dextrin, maltose, and glucose—the amount of the last depending on the time of boiling. The longer the period, the greater the amount of glucose. It is interesting to note that, as is shown in the chapter on brewing, that certain classes of enzymes are also able to bring about the conversion of starch into maltose, while others carry on the process a step further, replacing the maltose by glucose. The starchy matter chosen varies ; maize probably provides the greatest proportion. The obtaining of the starch is essentially a mechanical process, separating it from the nitrogenous and fatty matters in the corn. The prepared starch, intimately mixed with some of the dilute acid, is added to the other portion of the acid when boiling. The whole was formerly boiled in an open vessel. But open converters are now abandoned in favour of closed vessels strong enough to stand a pressure of five to six atmospheres. Steam is admitted under pressure, and the process carried on until chemical tests show that the starch has been converted. This may take place in about an hour and a half. The sulphuric acid has been acting as a catalyst, and therefore, not altering in amount, has to be removed after the operation. This is carried out by neutralizing it by means of an addition of whiting or chalk. This results in the formation of the rather insoluble sulphate of lime, which is allowed to settle to the bottom of the vessel, and removed by filtration. Much of the dissolved gluten is precipitated during the neutralizing, and forms a greenish scum. The clear liquid is boiled down further, and more sulphate of lime crystallizes out, leaving a syrup which is clarified, as in the case of sugar refining, by percolating through a vessel containing bone charcoal. The syrup is then evaporated in vacuum pans until semi-solid, and allowed to cool, usually after running into moulds. Glucose so obtained is a hard, opaque substance, varying in colour from white to pale yellow. Such a glucose will contain more or less traces of dextrin and maltose, the intermediate products between starch and glucose. A so-called glucose is manufactured in large quantities in this country, and used by brewers. It is an incompletely converted starch, and hence may contain anything up to from 50 to 66 per cent. of dextrin and maltose.

The well-known occurrence some years ago of arsenic in beer was due to the arsenic present in glucose. This impurity in the sugar was derived from the sulphuric acid used in its manufacture. Glucose is used extensively in confectionery, jam-making, medicine, and table syrup.

Foremost among the many sweetening agents brought into prominence during the Great War is saccharin. Like many another synthetic product of modern times, it is derived from coal tar, having for its starting-point the hydrocarbon toluene. The pure product has a sweetening power over 500 times that of cane sugar ; but the commercial quality may only be about 300 times as sweet. Enormous quantities are used in making mineral waters and ice cream, and as a substitute in the diet of patients suffering from diabetes.

The question as to whether saccharin is a dangerous drug has not been answered definitely one way or another. It was discovered by Remsen and Fahlberg in 1879.

CHAPTER X.

THE relationship of the various fermentation industries is extremely close when investigated from a chemical point of view. The ingredient common to beer, spirits, wines, and similar beverages is alcohol. There is a large number of alcohols known, and this one in particular is termed "ethyl alcohol." It is produced in these liquids through the agency of enzymes (Chapter I.), certain of which, apparently, have the ability to cause various sugars to break up into alcohol and carbonic acid gas. Enzymes, you will remember, belong to the group of substances termed catalysts, and in the fermentation industries they hold supreme sway, and control the direction of the processes. In certain cases the sugars which are converted into alcohol are present naturally ; but in others they may have been produced from starchy materials through the agency of other enzymes. As a rule, then, in the manufacture of these beverages we have starches transformed into sugars, passing *en route* through the substances called dextrins, and finally the sugars converted into alcohol. With this explanation let us turn to the consideration of one of the oldest of industries—namely, the brewing of beer.

The use of beer as a beverage stretches so far into the distant past, that its origin is still a debatable subject. Some writers produce evidence to show that the Egyptians as far back as 3000 B.C. made a beer or wine from corn as well as a wine from the grape. There is no doubt, however, that it was widely manufactured and consumed by all the Celtic peoples on the Continent prior to the fifth century; and by that period in this country, from being the occasional beverage of the wealthy, beer had become the general drink of all classes, being part of a breakfast or a supper, as tea and coffee are at present. It is worthy of note that previous to the sixteenth century the beer or ale contained no hops. Up to the eighteenth century vast numbers of people brewed their own beer, but the manufacture later gradually passed into the hands of the public brewer.

From time to time beer has appeared under such names as ale, stout, and porter. The origin of the word porter is ascribed to the fact that about 1720 a special quality was introduced which specially appealed to the labouring classes and porters. In the early part of the nineteenth century it constituted the great bulk of beer drunk in London.

In brewing, the nature of the water is of the utmost importance, and affects to a considerable extent the quality of the resulting beer. In fact the geographical positions of the great brewing centres have largely been determined by the available water supply. Burton-on-Trent has long been celebrated for its pale ales, while Dublin and London stand un-rivalled for the excellence of their stouts and porters. The reason for this difference lies in the various mineral constituents found dissolved in the respective water supplies. Burton water contains a large amount of calcium sulphate in solution, while that of Dublin, after boiling, gives a soft water—in other words, a water containing practically nothing in solution. Scientific investigation has now made it clear that hard waters containing calcium sulphate and a little magnesium sulphate are suitable for making pale ales, while soft waters give excellent stouts and porters. A chemical analysis now enables the modern brewer to modify many water supplies, so that they may become suitable for brewing the different types of beer. By the addition of the required mineral substances soft waters may be hardened and hard waters made soft. As a result it is now possible in the one locality, and using the same water, to produce both pale ales and stouts of high quality. It is also most important that the water should reach a high degree of organic purity—that is, it must be free from impurities resulting from the decomposition of animal or vegetable matter. Lastly, neither must it contain to any extent micro-organisms, and more especially those micro-organisms which are capable of development in beer.

The first step in the brewing of beer is the conversion of barley into malt. As a preliminary the barley is cleaned by means of separating sieves, and dust is removed by means of a current of air. Foreign seeds and broken corns are separated out, and the barley finally may be graded. The barley is allowed to steep in water for various periods, ranging from fifty to ninety hours, during which time water is absorbed by the grain. The barley begins to germinate, and for this function requires air. To ensure this being supplied, air may be directly blown into the steep, or the aeration may be effected by changing the water of the steep several times. The barley is then spread over floors, and made up to a good depth to encourage germination. When this has commenced the grain is more thinly spread.

Great care is taken that the temperature does not rise too high. This is usually secured by the turning over of the grain every three or five hours. The period on the floor may be anything from seven to fourteen days. The chemical actions taking place in the barley grain as it germinates or malts are exceedingly complex, and even yet have not been completely elucidated. The barley, as it malts on the floor, germinates; little rootlets appear, and the plumule, or acrospire, begins to grow. Simultaneously several of that class of bodies called enzymes are working with considerable energy within the grain. This consists chiefly of starch enclosed in cell walls. One of the enzymes named cytase attacks and destroys the cell walls, leaving the contents open to the invasion of a second enzyme, diastase, whose mission is to convert the starch into an important class of substance named dextrins. But when this stage is reached it does not cease its activities. It proceeds, and converts as many of these dextrins as it is allowed, by those controlling the operation, into the sugar called maltose. Through the influence of diastase we have present the maltose and the intermediate dextrins. A third enzyme, or group of enzymes, breaks down the complex nitrogenous bodies or proteids, forming others of simpler composition. As soon as these various modifications are sufficiently complete, which is usually the case when the plumule has grown nearly the length of the corn, further action is stopped by drying the malt in kilns. This is a very important operation, as the temperature and manner of drying have a far-reaching effect on the malt produced, and hence on the resulting beer. For example, the temperature must not be allowed to rise too high, or the enzymes will be destroyed, and their help is required afterwards by the brewer. Before being stored in bins the dried rootlets, or " culms " as they are termed, are removed from the malt.

The mashing operation next takes up our attention. The method of mashing adopted in this country is termed the infusion system. The malt is crushed, an endeavour being made to get the husks left fairly complete while the contents of the corn are in a very fine condition. The crushed malt (grist) is mixed with water and run into the mash tun, or the admixture may be made directly in the tun itself. Here, again, the temperatures of the malt and water are matters of considerable moment. In the mash tun the enzymes continue their activities, and as a result practically all the starch is broken up into dextrins and maltose, and the more complex proteids resolved into simpler bodies.

In many cases it is now customary to add to the mash tun other starch containing substances which will be converted along with the malt starch by the diastase of the malt. Maize, rice, and sometimes barley itself are utilized in this way. As a rule the starch of such bodies is first gelatinized by heating them, with or without a little malt, in an apparatus called a converter. The starch in the gelatinized state is more easily attacked by the diastase of the malt.

Rakes in the mash tun keep the contents well mixed, the operation usually being concluded in about an hour. The aqueous extract, or " wort " as it is termed, is then run from the mash tun to the copper, where it is boiled. The husks of the malt, if they have been left unbroken, help the drainage of the wort. During the draining process hot water is sprayed or sparged on the mass, to remove all the soluble matter. Again, the temperature of the sparging water has to be carefully looked after.

The wort is next boiled in the copper with the addition of hops. Various reactions take place. The liquid is concentrated ; further action by the enzymes is checked, as boiling destroys them ; the liquid is sterilized by destruction of the bacteria which have survived the mashing process ; a portion of the proteids is coagulated ; and the valuable constituents of the hops extracted which gives the beer its flavour, and which at the same time help to preserve and keep it sound for a longer period. The period during which the copper is boiled has been reduced within late years, and may now be taken on an average as one and a half to two hours. As a rule the copper is heated in this country by a direct fire; but in other centres steam heating has to some extent been adopted. At the conclusion of the boiling operation the wort is run into a vessel called a hop-back, which, being furnished with a perforated bottom, retains the hops and allows the clear wort to run through. From the hop-back the wort passes to the coolers, which consist of shallow tanks. The liquid lies in these to the depth of only a few inches. Not only does cooling take place in these, but at the same time the liquid gets thoroughly exposed to the air, which should be as pure as possible, the temperature of the wort being at this part of the process in many cases favourable for the development of bacteria. The cooling is usually completed in water cooled refrigerators, and the wort finally passes on to the fermentation vats.

The temperature of the wort having been reduced to approximately 60° F., yeast is added and the contents of the vat thoroughly mixed. The addition of the yeast, which must be healthy and vigorous, is termed " pitching." Yeast is a living organism, and if examined by a microscope will be found to consist of a great number of very small bodies roughly spherical in contour. In this country the yeast during fermentation makes its way to the surface, and gives rise to the term " top fermentation." On the Continent the yeasts employed in the manufacture of lager beer fall to the bottom of the vat, hence the term " bottom fermentation." During the fermenting process the yeast reproduces itself either by budding or by the formation of internal spores. Accordingly more yeast is secured at the end of the operation than was employed for pitching.

The nature of the actions taking place during fermentation was for long misunderstood. It was eventually proved that the activity of the yeast was due to it containing an enzyme named "zymase," which breaks up the sugars in the wort into alcohol and carbonic acid gas. Small amounts of glycerine and succinic acid are produced simultaneously. The modern explanation also demands the presence of a co-enzyme and certain alkaline phosphates. The yeast cell requires free oxygen for its growth and development, and certain substances must be present in the wort for its nutrition. Such are the sugars, certain nitrogenous substances, phosphates, and, finally, salts of potash. In certain cases so-called yeast foods containing these substances are added to the wort, if it is concluded that the wort is deficient in these.

The yeast employed by the British brewer is not a single variety of pure culture, but usually contains more than one type. On the Continent Professor E. C. Hansen introduced pure cultures, and one may find several different yeasts employed, each of which will produce a different class of beer.

During fermentation the temperature of the liquid in the vats is not allowed to rise too high. This is accomplished by means of attemperators, consisting of pipes through which cold water can be run. On conclusion of the action the yeast is skimmed off or removed by some other system in vogue, and the beer " racked " or run into casks and set aside to mature. A small quantity of dry hops may be added at this stage. This dry hopping, for which the finest hops are usually employed, gives the beer a pleasant hop aroma.

At the moment the beer is transferred to the cask the fermentation has spent itself, and the beer would become flat and undrinkable were it not for the fact that a different race of yeast takes the work upon itself. This type attacks and ferments substances in the beer which were not attacked during the so-called primary fermentation. They are known as secondary or " wild " yeasts, and are often introduced into the beer from the hops or from the air itself. During the brewing processes they are seldom absent, but have hitherto been kept in check by the stronger primary yeast. Very often the beer in the cask is turbid owing to the suspension in it of yeast cells, proteids, etc. If it is in that condition it is usual to clear it by the addition of a viscous solution of isinglass in either tartaric or sulphurous acid. This operation is termed " finding." The isinglass, taking with it the suspended matter, is either carried out of the bung-hole by the carbonic acid gas, or sinks to the bottom of the cask—in any case leaving the beer clear.

A comparatively recent development in the practice of brewing is the introduction of a process of chilling, filtering, and carbonating ales. The chilling causes certain matters to separate from the beer which might cause turbidity. Filtering cold, we obtain a bright beer. In brewing great care must be given to cleanliness of vessels and plant to avoid contamination through bacteria and certain wild yeasts. Alcohol and the hop resins are bactericidal to a certain extent, but certain bacteria can thrive in such a medium. In this category are included the acetic acid bacteria, which turn the beer sour. In the case of strong beers, in which there is a larger percentage of alcohol, the difficulty of keeping beer sound is not so great.

The by-products of the brewing industry are of some importance. First of all we have the spent grain very largely used as a cattle food. Probably next in importance is the carbonic acid gas produced during fermentation. This is collected, purified, and sold to mineral water manufacturers; it is also used to drive torpedoes and for extinguishing fires. It is doubtful whether it should be regarded as a by-product nowadays, for a large number of breweries use it for the gassing of their own beer, the demand for carbonated beer in bottle being largely on the increase. Yeast is another by-product. Under ordinary conditions, if one pound of yeast is used to " pitch," about five or six pounds will be recovered. It is used as a cattle food, and also by chemical treatment it can be converted into a paste which can hardly be distinguished from meat extract. Mixed with distillers' yeast, it is proposed to use the brewery product in bread-making. The spent hops, after drying, are utilized as a nitrogenous manure.

Some of the earliest researches in brewing were made by Pasteur, who published in 1876 his " Studies on Beer." He investigated the maladies which affected beer, and traced them to the microscopic organisms or bacteria which introduce themselves invisibly into it. From those he was led to the study of infectious diseases; and very few, even including medical men, have any real conception that the true source of bacteriology, with the incalculable benefits derived by its application, was the brewing industry. Antiseptic surgery was also the direct outcome of Pasteur's work, and modern surgery, like preventative medicine, is a child of the fermentation industries. Lord Lister, learning of Pasteur's work on alcoholic and lactic fermentations, in which the phenomena of fermentation and putrefaction were definitely connected with the presence of micro-organisms, was led to associate the suppuration of open wounds with the action of these organisms coming from without. Inspired with this idea he commenced treatment, which gradually led to the triumphs of aseptic surgery.

CHAPTER XI.

OTHER FERMENTATION INDUSTRIES : INDUSTRIAL
ALCOHOL.

GROUPED under this heading we have the manufacture of the various liquids containing alcohol, such as wines, whisky, brandy, rum, gin, cider, and industrial alcohol. In addition, the title may be taken as including the preparation of vinegar. From the time of Noah, the first victim of the grape, men have drunk liquids containing ethyl alcohol, and in spite of practically all the Governments of the world levying ever-increasing taxes on alcoholic beverages, their consumption has at no time materially decreased. Arguing from premises such as these, several writers have endeavoured to prove that alcohol is the normal drink of man. On the other hand, the alcohol present in whisky and its companion beverages may be extracted by processes of distillation, and, so prepared, constitutes a substance whose chemical properties, solvent powers, and ʻheating value make it, next to water, the most valuable liquid known.

Wines.—Like beer, wines are of remote origin, fermented grape juice being the beverage of the ancient Egyptians. We have it on record that at several celebrated feasts given in the fifth century pledges were made with golden bowls filled with wine, which, since Britain was not a wine-making country, must have been imported.

Even before the Norman Conquest the wine trade with France was of considerable importance. Claret was largely sold in England, licences being granted to drapers, tailors, fishmongers, and various other tradespeople. The consumption of wine enormously increased, and even under the Puritans its use was practically unchecked. For some time during the French wars, and after, the importation of French wines decreased, and other varieties became more popular. This decrease had its origin in the hatred of all things French, and was also due to the fact that the import duties on claret were raised to £55 per ton, compared with £7 per ton on Portuguese wine. In France wine is looked upon as a temper-ance drink, the average Frenchman being accustomed to take wine as an ordinary everyday beverage.

The great wine-producing countries are France, Spain, Portugal, and Germany, while the Argentine and Australian vintages are also of importance. The Australian wines are named after the European varieties, appearing under such names as " sherry," " port," and so on. Wines are produced from the fermentation of the juice of the grape. The juice contains glucose and other sugars ; the amounts of those and of the other constituents vary in quantity according to the kind of grape and the nature of the soil and climate.

Unlike the brewing of beer, the yeast which brings

about the conversion of the sugars into alcohol and carbonic acid gas is not added, but is derived from the " bloom " covering the outsides of the skins.

The grapes are crushed, and the juice extracted by pressing, or, better, in centrifugal machines. Red wines owe their colour to the husks of the grapes, which are retained, whereas in white wines they are removed. In Champagne the fruit is gathered before maturity, while in Burgundy the grapes are vintaged when they are showing the greatest colour.

In a few hours after being put into the fermenting vats the clear juice, or "must," becomes turbid; soon a rapid evolution of carbonic acid gas begins, and a froth forms on the surface. Eventually the yeast settles, and as the alcohol content increases, a deposit of argol takes place; this is the source of the cream of tartar of commerce. When the liquid becomes clear it is drawn off into large casks, the bungs closed, and it is allowed to ripen.

As a rule the strongest wines made by fermentation do not contain more than from 16 to 17 per cent. of alcohol, a greater amount of alcohol stopping the fermenting action. Such liquids are in many cases fortified by the addition of alcohol produced by the distillation of other wines. For example, port wine is fortified with brandy, which is the alcoholic distillate from wine.

Whisky.—Whisky is the national drink of Scotland and Ireland. The word itself came into vogue at the end of the eighteenth century, and is derived from the Celtic " usquebaugh."

There being some doubt as to what whisky really

is, a Royal Commission in 1908–9 defined it as " a spirit obtained by distillation from a mash of cereal grains saccharified by the diastase of malt. That Scotch whisky is whisky distilled in Scotland, and Irish whisky is whisky distilled in Ireland." Whisky, like beer, is made from malted barley or from a mixture of malted barley and some other starchy material. The chief difference between the two processes consists in the longer time the diastase is allowed to act on the starch. In brewing, the starch is converted into dextrin and maltose, of which only the maltose is capable of being afterwards fermented ; hence the alcohol content of beer is comparatively slow. In the case of whisky the prolonged action of the diastase converts practically all the starch into maltose, and in consequence a greater amount of alcohol is produced at fermentation. After fermentation and removal of the yeast the liquid is distilled either in a " pot " still or in a " patent " still. In the case of the pot still two distillations are made. The first distillate is termed " low wines." This is subjected to a second distillation, and the volatile liquids condensed and collected in several fractions. The first fraction coming over is termed " foreshoots," while the third portion is called " feints." These are added to the next quantity of liquid which is about to undergo distillation. The second fraction is the liquid familiar to us under the term " whisky." The various characters of the different whiskies are due to the $\frac{1}{2}$ per cent. of ether and higher alcohols present.

In a patent still a more efficient separation of

the alcohol and the secondary constituents is brought about, resulting in a spirit which approximates more to pure alcohol than pot-still whisky. Most of the patent-still whisky is blended with pot-still whisky, from which it derives the whisky flavour. The spirit is stored in sherry casks, and owing to the more rapid diffusion of the alcohol through the wood, an increase of secondary constituents takes place. Certain products are oxidized and so destroyed during ageing in the cask, and numerous processes have been suggested to artificially age the whisky. Such methods depend upon the action of some oxidizing agent.

Gin is made similarly from barley, and flavoured with juniper; while rum is produced by fermenting molasses, and then distilling. Brandy and cognac, on the other hand, are the distillates from wine.

Industrial Alcohol.—On the commercial scale, alcohol is obtained from potatoes, maize, rice, rye, etc.—in fact, from any substance which contains either sugar or starch. Bad grain and rotting fruit may be utilized as raw material, while in recent years more or less successful endeavours have been made to produce it from sawdust. In Germany the potato is the chief source of supply, and it is interesting to note that during the Great War, as potatoes became more and more necessary as foodstuff, Germany was found to be importing an increasing amount of wine *via* Denmark and the other neutral countries. The alcohol was extracted from the wine and employed in the manufacture of explosives. In the manufacture of alcohol the potatoes are rasped and crushed. Malt is then added, so that its diastase may convert the potato starch into maltose. The water extract, or wort, is fermented as in brewing, and the alcohol obtained from the resulting liquid by distillation in a patent still.

Most countries at the present time make a distinction in taxation between alcohol used as a beverage and alcohol used for industrial purposes. But difficulty at once arises from the necessity to see that no alcohol intended for industrial purposes is used for bibulous purposes. This is usually done by enacting that tax free alcohol for use in manufacture shall be mixed with certain substances which will make it impossible to drink. In losing its character as a beverage it is said to be " denatured." There is no ideal substance employed as yet for this purpose, despite the great amount of work done on the question. It must be intolerable to the stomach, cheap, not easily removed from the alcohol, and, lastly, must not interfere with the industrial purposes it is intended for. The usual denaturants are the spirit obtained by distillation of wood, benzine, and pyridine.

Methylated spirit consists of ninety parts of alcohol denatured by the addition of ten parts of crude wood spirit and a little paraffin oil. In some cases it has been necessary to authorize special denaturants for special purposes. Camphor is utilized in the celluloid industry, hence the celluloid manufacturer is permitted to denature with camphor.

Some of the industrial uses of alcohol depend upon its solvent powers. It is used to dissolve or " cut " shellac, and is hence employed in all those innumerable articles on which men use varnish: so also in the manufacture of lacquers, in the production of dyes, fine chemicals—in short, hardly an industry but makes use of it. Large amounts are consumed in the manufacture of explosives, and the output of alcohol from the distilleries in the United Kingdom was an important factor in the Great War.

Not only is it useful on its own account, but it is important as the source of other substances, such as chloroform and ether. Considerable attention has also been devoted to its employment as a source of heat and of motive power. In the latter case it would be used as a substitute for petrol.

Cider.—Apples are gathered in as dry a condition as possible, and stored preferably under cover. During the period of storage the apples ripen and the percentage of sugar increases considerably. The fruit loses water by transpiration, so in that way a concentration of juice occurs. From the chemical point of view the period of storage is a critical one.

For the preparation of the cider, the fruit is put into a " grater " type of mill, which rapidly reduces it to a very fine pulp. This pulp, or " pomace," as it is generally termed, is then subjected to a steady pressure which expresses the juice. With an efficient press the yield of juice should average about 80 per cent. of the original weight of fruit. Exposed in an open vessel, various yeasts from the air and skins of the fruit cause the juice to ferment, producing alcohol and carbonic acid gas from the sugars present. Some experiments have been made with selected yeasts, but the results on the whole have been disappointing. Fermentation is usually stopped by filtration, the point of cessation depending whether a sweet cider or dry cider is desired. If the sweet variety is required, the fermentation is checked before all the sugar has undergone conversion into alcohol.

Cider is increasing in popularity as a beverage, and in this country about 100 million gallons are manufactured yearly. Orchards for the growth of cider apples are attached, as a rule, to most farms in the west of England.

Vinegar.—Next to the alcoholic fermentation in technical importance is the fermentation caused by a group of bacteria bringing about the formation of acetic acid. The micro-organisms convert alcohol into acetic acid with the assistance of the atmospheric oxygen.

The chief materials employed in vinegar manufacture are cider and decoctions made from malt. The fermentation is usually carried out in tall vats or casks. These have perforated false bottoms, on which rest the filling of beachwood shavings, reaching nearly to the top of the cask. The shavings are soaked in strong vinegar before filling into the vat, and are covered with a film of the ferment. Starting from malt, the manufacturer ferments his water extract of malt as far as possible by means of yeast, and allows the resulting dilute solution of alcohol to percolate through the shavings. The temperature of the vat rises as the liquid comes in contact with the ferment on the shavings, and causes air to rise through the vessel. A very exact regulation of the strength and flow of alcoholic liquid, and of the amount of air admitted, is essential to proper working. After acetification the vinegar is transferred to store vats, and kept until ready for dilutions to the strength required by the trade.

The colour of the vinegar (white or brown) depends upon the temperature at which the original malt was dried. The highly dried malts, being darker, give a deeper colour to the vinegar. Such vinegars also contain phosphates and other extractive matters. Imitation vinegar is often made from dilute acetic acid, which is one of the substances produced when wood is distilled. This is coloured with caramel, and flavouring matter added, but usually contains neither phosphates nor other matters characteristic of true vinegar.

CHAPTER XII.

SOME INDUSTRIAL USES OF THE RARE EARTHS.

MORE than one-half of the chemical elements are extremely rare, being very seldom worked at, even by chemists, and absolutely unheard-of by the layman. Such are the rare earths. They form a group by themselves, and are so much alike in properties that special and laborious methods are required for their separation. In some cases the designation " rare " is now a misnomer. Thoria and ceria, the more important of these earths, were very seldom met with at one time, and the sources of supply were strictly limited. But as the demand for these and similar substances grew, new deposits were brought to light, and some of the earths which were formerly considered as rare have now been found to occur in certain parts of the world in amounts which are practically inexhaustible.

The principal consumers of certain of the rare earths are the incandescent gas mantle manufacturers. It is common knowledge that the introduction of solid matter into a non-luminous flame causes emission of light. Lime is a common example of a substance possessing this property; the well-known " limelight " being the result of heating a lime cylinder to incandescence in a flame produced by the combustion of coal gas in oxygen. Some of the rarer earths were known to impart an even greater brilliance to the flame, and the researches of Baron Auer von Welsbach put on a practical basis some of the former well-known facts. He was struck with the idea that a cotton fabric impregnated with certain of these earths and suspended in a gas flame might be used for practical lighting. After laborious investigation, he eventually found that the greatest illumination was given by a mixture containing 99 per cent. of thoria and 1 per cent. of ceria. A great deal of discussion has arisen as to the exact part played by the small quantity of ceria, and why such a mixture should display greater illumination powers than the pure thoria. Although Welsbach first invented the rare-earth mantle in 1886, it was not until 1893 that it became a commercial success. Objections were soon found to cotton as the fabric, and systematic search was made for other materials. Ramie, or China grass, now grown in India and Italy, was discovered to be almost ideal for the purpose. Artificial silk is to some extent being employed to replace the ramie yarn, and gives a mantle combining the high and well-maintained illuminating power of the ramie yarn with a greater elasticity of ash skeleton.

The thoria and ceria are found in small amounts in monazite sand. Although monazite sand occurs in many localities all over the world, the only deposits of commercial importance are those on the coast of Brazil and in Travancore, India. The latter sand is of greater value, containing a higher content of thoria. Prior to 1903 Germany obtained large quantities of the sand at a small cost owing to its being shipped as ballast. In that year, however, the Brazilian Government discovered the value of the mineral, and leased the rights to work most of the deposits eventually to the German Thorium Syndicate. The deposits at Travancore, after an unsuccessful attempt to obtain the capital to work them in the United Kingdom, were also sold to a German firm. As a result, the incandescent mantle manufacturers in this country were almost entirely dependent upon German supplies—a state of affairs which lasted until shortly after the outbreak of the Great War. An official investigation was made in the case of the Travancore sand, with the result that enemy interests were eliminated, German contracts cancelled, and an arrangement made for the future control to be in the hands of British-born subjects. During 1916–17 a large proportion of the Travancore output was sold to the United States of America.

The crude sand contains only a small amount of monazite. Accordingly it is customary to concentrate the sand by sluicing away much of the lighter material, and by electro-magnetic separation, so that it contains from 85 to 90 per cent. of monazite. In this concentrated condition thoria constitutes, at the most, only about 9 per cent., and the cerium earths about 60 per cent., of the sand.

The extraction of thoria and ceria from these sands is only possible after a very complicated series of operations. They eventually reach the market in the form of thorium nitrate and cerium nitrate, both substances being soluble in water.

The first step in the manufacture of the mantle consists in knitting a continuous cylindrical hose. Cotton and ramie mantles must be washed before impregnation, in order to remove the fat and mineral matter in the yarn. The mineral matters, if not removed, are left in the ash skeleton after burning off the vegetable fibre, and bring about a reduction of the luminosity. Their removal may be accomplished in various ways. Digesting overnight in a 2 per cent. solution of nitric acid, drying, and then treating with a dilute solution of ammonia followed by thorough washing, brings about their satisfactory elimination. The fabric is dried in a hot air chamber, and subsequently cut up in a cutting-machine into pieces of equal length. The mantles are impregnated by soaking in an aqueous solution of thorium and cerium nitrates, in the proportion of 99 to 1, to which very small quantities of the nitrates of magnesium and beryllium are added to harden and impart strength to the ash skeleton. One or two minutes' soaking is sufficient for ramie, while artificial silk requires five hours. The superfluous solution of the nitrates is removed by passing through a wringing machine, furnished with gutta-percha rollers, carefully adjusted to leave the correct quantity of nitrate in the mantle. The mantles are next stretched over glass cylinders, and dried at a temperature not exceeding 30° c.

The upright mantles are then fitted with a sewn-on tulle head, which is soaked with the aqueous solution, but containing a slightly greater percentage of the hardening salts. Finally, the asbestos loop is sewn on. In the case of the inverted mantles they are drawn together with impregnated cotton to form the " spider," and then fastened to the supporting ring. At this stage of the operation the manufacturer may satisfy his natural desire to advertise the excellence of his goods by painting a label on the mantle. This is usually done with a solution of didymium salts, so that in the heat of the burner his name will shine forth from the incandescent background of the mantle.

The next operation consists in burning off the fibre, and at the same time decomposing the nitrates into the oxides, thoria and ceria. This is carried out while the mantle is hung on an iron hook and placed in an intensely hot flame. The fibre disappears, and what is left is a kind of fragile pottery, a delicate filament of oxides preserving faithfully the original pattern of the fabric. There still remains one thing more to do. It must be strengthened to endure transport from the works to the houses of the users. This is ensured by dipping the ash skeleton into a collodion solution, which usually contains collodion, ether, camphor, and castor-oil. After drying rapidly at from 50° to 60° c, the mantles are trimmed, and the imperfect ones rejected.

The rings on which the inverted mantles are supported are composed of china clay, sand, and magnesia, worked into a plastic state with oil. They are shaped in a model die, and fired in a pottery furnace.

During 1913 the estimated consumption of incandescent gas mantles in the United Kingdom amounted to about 100 millions, and of these approximately 60 millions, valued at nearly £200,000, were imported from Germany. In addition, thorium nitrate to the value of £41,544 was also imported. In other words, practically no thorium nitrate was being made in the United Kingdom from monazite sand, the only production being from waste mantle ash. The amount of the thorium nitrate obtained from this source probably amounted to one-fifth of the country's requirements. It is satisfactory, however, to record that at least four British mantle manufacturers are now making the nitrate in sufficient quantity for their requirements.

There are several other industries which use fair quantities of ceria and its allied rare earths. Chief among them is the employment of cerium in the manufacture of pyrophoric alloys. As already mentioned, thoria at most constitutes only about 9 per cent. of the monazite sand, while ceria and its allies form about 60 per cent. And as the gas mantle contained only 1 per cent. of ceria to 99 per cent. of thoria, enormous quantities of these cerium earths accumulated at the chemical works where thorium nitrate was prepared. Many endeavours were made by chemists to find a profitable method of utilizing this waste product. Here again we owe the discovery to Welsbach. When the by-product oxides were reduced, a mixture of metals (mainly cerium) is obtained. Welsbach took advantage of the fact that the metals, when filed, gave off a shower of sparks, which in turn was able to ignite a combustible gas or vapour. Better results were obtained when the metals were alloyed with about 30 per cent. of iron. The sparking substance in the majority of automatic cigar lighters consists of this ferro-cerium or cerium-pyrophoric alloy. The amount of alloy used in each light is exceedingly small, about 2,500 pieces going to make one pound.

Another part played by ferro-cerium is to be seen in its use as a " tracer " of the flight of shells. A small piece of the alloy is affixed to the shell, and during the flight of the projectile the friction of the air generates sufficient heat as to cause the alloy to burst into flame, and so indicate the path of the shell. These alloys were made in this country by a German firm, from materials imported from Germany. At the present time the supply is coming from the United States.

Welsbach disposed of his original patent for making the alloy for £30,000 to a company which monopolized the market for a number of years; but later the patent was disputed, and its operation was limited.

INDEX.